The Travels of Increase Joseph

A Historical Novel about a Pioneer Preacher

Jerry Apps

Terrace Books
A trade imprint of the University of Wisconsin Press

Books by Jerry Apps

Fiction:
The Travels of Increase Joseph
In a Pickle
Blue Shadows Farm
Cranberry Red

Nonfiction:
The Land Still Lives
Cabin in the Country
Barns of Wisconsin
Mills of Wisconsin and the Midwest
Breweries of Wisconsin
One-Room Country Schools
Wisconsin Traveler's Companion
Country Wisdom
Cheese: The Making of a Wisconsin Tradition
When Chores Were Done
Country Ways and Country Days
Humor from the Country
The People Came First: A History of Cooperative Extension
Ringlingville USA
Every Farm Tells a Story
Living a Country Year
Old Farm: A History
Horse Drawn Days

Audio Books:
The Back Porch and Other Stories
In a Pickle

Children's Books:
Eat Rutabagas
Stormy
Tents, Tigers, and the Ringling Brothers
Casper Jaggi: Master Swiss Cheese Maker

For Steve

Terrace Books, a trade imprint of the University of Wisconsin
Press, takes its name from the Memorial Union Terrace, located at
the University of Wisconsin–Madison. Since its inception in 1907,
the Wisconsin Union has provided a venue for students, faculty,
staff, and alumni to debate art, music, politics, and the issues of the
day. It is a place where theater, music, drama, literature, dance,
outdoor activities, and major speakers are made available to the
campus and the community. To learn more about the Union,
visit www.union.wisc.edu.

Terrace Books
A trade imprint of the University of Wisconsin Press
1930 Monroe Street, 3rd Floor
Madison, Wisconsin 53711-2059
uwpress.wisc.edu

3 Henrietta Street
London WC2E 8LU, England
www.eurospanbookstore.com

5 4 3 2 1

Printed in the United States of America

Library of Congress Cataloging-in-Publication Data
Apps, Jerold W., 1934–
    The travels of Increase Joseph: a historical novel about a
pioneer preacher / Jerry Apps.
      p.   cm.
    ISBN 978-0-299-24754-6 (pbk.: alk. paper)—
    ISBN 978-0-299-24753-9 (e-book)
    1. Frontier and pioneer life—Fiction. 2. Wisconsin—Fiction.
3. Lightning—Fiction. 4. Clergy—Fiction. I. Title.
PS3601.P67T73   2010
813′.6—dc22
                                                2009050424

This is a work of fiction. Any resemblance to actual persons or
events are purely coincidental. Historical persons and events are
used in a fictional context.

Contents

The Truth of the Matter

Although this is a work of fiction, the historical setting for the story is true, as are some of the characters and many of the circumstances. There was no Increase Joseph Link, but there was an Increase Lapham, after whom the main character was named. Increase Lapham, as one writer noted, was "Wisconsin's pioneer scientist and scholar and a true Renaissance man."

In an earlier book, *Village of Roses* (1973), I wrote about the Standalone Church that stood for several years south of present day Wild Rose, Wisconsin. As the locals then reported, "the Standalones did some strange things," but their doings have little or no resemblance to the Standalone Fellowship that I describe.

Many early settlers came to Wisconsin via Buffalo, New York, and the Great Lakes. Sheboygan was a popular port in the 1850s for settlers seeking land in central Wisconsin. Sylvanus and Betsy Wade operated Wade House in Greenbush for many years. This was a popular stopping place for people traveling the rugged plank road from Sheboygan to Fond du Lac.

In the 1850s and beyond, Berlin, Wisconsin, on the Fox River, was a popular trading post both for Native Americans as well as pioneers. For several years Native Americans brought their furs to Berlin, where they traded for salt, blankets, and a variety of other products.

There is no Link Lake, nor is there an Ames County in Wisconsin and thus there was no *Link Lake Gazette.* There were, however, many local newspapers in Wisconsin including the *Marinette and Peshtigo Eagle* that was edited by Luther B. Noyes.

The land in Central Wisconsin where this story takes place once was Menominee Indian land. The treaty, which turned over thousands of acres to the U.S. government, was signed at Lake Poygan, not far from Oshkosh, in 1848. One of the chiefs to sign the treaty was indeed Kee-chee-new.

From settlement days until the 1870s, much of central and southern Wisconsin was devoted to wheat growing. Farming practices depicted in this book were accurate for that time. Drought and devastating sandstorms were not uncommon.

Several black families settled in Cheyenne Valley, today Vernon County, where they successfully farmed. One of the community leaders was Walden Stewart. Contour plowing (plowing around the hills) got its start in Vernon County.

Wisconsin was involved to a considerable extent with the Underground Railroad, although the situation depicted here is fictional. As most people know, Wisconsin's commitment to the Civil War was substantial. And it was possible for someone to buy his way out of serving in the Civil War, or he could try to persuade someone to take his place.

Northern Wisconsin was a vast timberland when the first settlers arrived. During the middle 1800s until the early 1900s, lumber companies logged off much of the northern timber, often leaving a wasteland studded with giant tree stumps. There is no Broadax, Wisconsin, but there were many lumber towns like it, scattered all through northern Wisconsin.

William Dempster Hoard, the founder of *Hoard's Dairyman* magazine, along with Chester Hazen and several others with New York roots, helped transform Wisconsin from a wheat growing state to a dairy state starting in the 1860s. Hoard went on to become governor of Wisconsin.

The 1871 Peshtigo Fire occurred much as described, with the loss of more than 1,200 lives, most of the buildings in the thriving city of Peshtigo, plus numerous farmsteads and thousands of acres of timberland.

John Deere's plow, Cyrus McCormick's reaper and J. I. Case's threshing machine and steam engines transformed much of Wisconsin's agriculture after the Civil War. The first barbed wire (1873) is credited to Joseph Glidden, a farmer from DeKalb, Illinois.

The 1893 World's Columbian Exposition is accurately described. This great World's Fair, although held during one of the country's severest depressions, drew thousands of people. This was clearly a watershed time for American society as electricity was introduced, along with carbonated soda water, the music of Scott Joplin, Shredded Wheat, Cream of Wheat, Juicy Fruit Gum and much more. More importantly, speakers at the fair proclaimed that technology was the future and that agrarian principles and practices must be relegated to history. No one at the fair likely said, "Technology is king and progress has become America's destiny," although this was certainly an underlying theme. Some questioned this headlong rush toward new technology. Although spoken by fictional character Little Joe, the words — "Progress is the religion of the machine, the ministry of big business, and the worship of want" — were expressed by a quiet minority.

Aside from the factual history, the story is fiction.

The Travels of
Increase Joseph

Chapter 1
Tossed Out

Plum Falls, New York
May 1848

He carried a dog-eared Holy Bible in one hand; the other held a brown tattered satchel containing his meager possessions. The satchel was tied together with a hank of frayed yellow rope. A floppy brown hat rode low on his head. Threadbare trousers came half way to his knees and the sleeves of his shirt, too short for long arms, crept part way to his elbows. With his head down, he walked slowly along the twisting country road toward his father's farm dimly seen in the distance. Badly worn shoes sent up little puffs of dust as he made his way, kicking the occasional gravel stone. After every few steps, he stopped, set down the worn satchel, retrieved a handkerchief from a back pocket and swabbed his sweating brow for it was a warm spring afternoon.

"Hal-low, that you Increase Joseph Link comin' down the road?" his mother called from the porch of their weathered farmhouse. She held her hand to her forehead, shielding her eyes from the bright sun. Her limp brown hair was damp with perspiration.

"It's me, Ma. It's me comin' down the road," Increase Joseph replied.

"College out early this year?" his mother called again. "Didn't expect you for a few more weeks."

"Comin' home early, Ma," Increase Joseph said. "Comin' home early." He stepped up on the porch and put down his satchel. A skinny brown dog, his ribs showing and his tail wagging, crawled from under the porch and thrust his nose into Increase Joseph's free hand.

"Why you comin' home early, son?"

"They tossed me out."

"Tossed ya out?"

"Yup, that's what they did. Said they didn't want to see me back either. Said I wasn't the kind of feller that would ever make a decent preacher."

"They said that did they?"

"Yup, that's what they said. I even asked if they'd consider changing their minds. They said no, they'd decided. And that was that."

Just then, Increase Joseph's father came from around the corner of the house. He was a grim looking, tall, balding, thin man wearing a straw hat and a gray homespun shirt and pants held up with suspenders.

"Sounded like you," he said. "Why ya home early son?"

"They tossed me out."

"Tossed you out?"

"Yup, that's what they did." Increase Joseph took off his hat and looked off across the recently plowed field of his father's farm.

"Why'd they toss you out, son?"

"Said I'd make the wrong kind of preacher."

"Wrong kinda preacher?"

"Yup." Increase Joseph's mother sat down on the edge of the porch. The other two soon joined her.

"Wrong kinda preacher?" Increase Joseph's father repeated in a louder voice.

"That's what they said, and that's why I'm here a couple weeks early."

For a time no one spoke. Increase Joseph patted the brown dog on the head and called him by name. The "thump, thump" of the dog's tail sounded like a ruffed grouse pounding its wings on a log.

"Well, you're here," Increase Joseph's mother said.

"Yup, I am," the young man answered.

"I think you should go back and tell them fellers at Harvard College off," Increase Joseph's father said. "You go back and tell 'em they don't know their ass-ends from a knot hole. It's what you outta do."

"Wouldn't help, Pa. Wouldn't help."

"Make you feel better. Tellin' them edjacated fellers what you think of 'em."

"I'm out Pa. No going back."

A gust of wind sent a little cloud of dust rolling along the country road. A meadowlark, sitting on a fence post alongside the newly plowed field, commenced to sing its spring song.

"Want me to go back there with you, to that stinkin' little college with its stuck-up teachers who think they got a corner on what preachin' is all about?"

"No, Pa. Wouldn't help if you came back there

with me."

"Sometimes I think you just ain't got any backbone, son. You let people walk right up yer skinny
frame and pound dust in yer ears. That's what
you do sometimes. Let people pound dust in yer
ears."

"Maybe so, Pa. Maybe so."

"Well by God, it just ain't right what them fellers
done to you. It ain't right!"

"It's too late, Pa. And your carrying on doesn't
help much. I already feel as low as a garter snake
crawling through cow manure."

"No sense in feelin' that way. You ought be
gettin' up your gander."

"Well, I do Pa. I feel bad. Feel bad all over. Had
my heart set on being a preacher."

"I know you did son. And you'd a made a fair to
middlin' one, too. Yes you would of. I know you
would of."

"Your father's right," his mother chimed in. She
had been sitting quietly, listening and running her
hands through her graying hair as she was prone
to do when she was upset. "You'd been better than
a fair to middlin' preacher. You'd been right up
there with them preacher fellers who keep a whole
field of people listenin' and prayin' and figurin'
out ways of improvin' their lives. You would of."

Increase Joseph reached over and touched his
mother on the arm.

Chapter 2
Lightning Strikes

June 1850

A dark cloud boiled up in the west and the distant rumble of thunder echoed across the valley as Increase Joseph Link slowly walked to fetch the milk cows from the night pasture. The rising sun, not yet above the horizon, streaked the eastern sky with reds and pinks. Link's farm dog, its long tail wagging slowly, followed Increase Joseph along the dusty cow path of his father's farm. The path started at the barn and trailed up the narrow lane, past the apple orchard, beyond the potato patch, and into the thin stand of oak trees where the cows spent the night.

The air hung heavy, as it often did just ahead of a storm. The smells of the early morning—dust, trampled grass, and cow manure—were thick and rich, but Increase Joseph, so accustomed to this early morning walk, paid no attention.

As he walked, Increase Joseph couldn't erase from his mind his dismissal from college, now more than two years ago. How he wanted to become a preacher of the faith, to stand before a crowd with his arms upraised allowing words of inspiration and forgiveness to tumble from his mouth. But this was not to be, and the reality had thrown him into a nearly constant depression.

He was happy for a time when he met Elwina Grabholtz, courted and married her. Elwina, 24, a plain farm girl with a prominent nose, dark brown eyes and wide shoulders, had nearly given up any chance of marrying. Then she met shy, seldom talking Increase Joseph Link. When he, in a moment of passionate confusion, suggested marriage, she quickly consented. From her perspective, and the perspective of many, he was no prize and in most courting contests he wouldn't be in the running. But she was desperate and the fellow, even with his many shortcomings, at least wore pants and knew something about farming.

To the great surprise of everyone in the community, Elwina gave birth to a baby boy hardly nine months later.

"Didn't think Increase Joseph knew about such things," a neighbor proclaimed. "Figured he thought beds were only for sleeping. Wonder what got into him? Or maybe the question was who got into her?" Folks couldn't believe that Increase Joseph Link was the father; yet, the little boy was a dead ringer for Increase Joseph. That single fact quelled further comment about the baby's lineage.

The sound of thunder grew louder as Increase Joseph neared the end of the farm lane and turned into the little stand of trees. He saw a jagged bolt of lightning cut across the black, boiling sky in front of him and a few seconds later heard the resounding roar of thunder. He pushed on, more quickly now, as he wanted to round up the cows and herd them back to the barn before the rain started. The bony dog rubbed up against Increase Joseph's leg and whined.

"What's a matter Ralph, thunder bothering you?" he said to the dog.

The dog shivered and whined again.

Increase Joseph stopped, stooped down and patted the dog's head.

"Just a thunderstorm, fellow. Just a little thunder. Be back to the barn as soon as we find those blame cows."

Increase Joseph awakened to find himself sprawled alongside the muddy cow path. His head ached furiously and there was a great ringing in his ears. He slowly focused his eyes and saw Ralph, his dog, lying alongside him, not moving, not breathing.

He staggered to his knees and then to his feet, trying to figure out what happened. He spotted jagged pieces of oak wood all around him. He looked toward a big oak tree a few feet in front of him and saw a jagged wound that started at the top of the tree, tore down its trunk, all the way to the ground.

Just then he saw his father coming up the cow path, hurrying.

"What happened to you son?" Then his father blurted out. "My god, your hair has turned white. Your hair is white, son."

Increase Joseph opened his mouth to speak, but he couldn't, he couldn't form the words. All that came out were a few grunts.

"Lightning," his father said. "You been struck

by lighting." The old man spotted the dog, dead by the trail. "Ralph sure was a good dog," he said. He grabbed the dog by the tail and pulled the animal back of the big oak tree with the slash down its side.

The senior Link supported his son as they slowly moved along the cow trail to the farmhouse where Increase Joseph shocked his mother and his wife with his appearance. His baby son took one look at his father and began screaming.

Increase Joseph's father immediately went to the pantry, brought out a jug of tonic, and poured full a glass of the amber liquid.

"Drink this," his father said.

Increase Joseph sat on the edge of the parlor couch, shaking his head back and forth and staring at the floor. His ghostly white hair flowed down over his shoulders.

The jug of tonic was only brought out during emergencies, severe illnesses or injuries. It was clear that this was an appropriate time. Increase Joseph lifted the glass of tonic to his lips, drained it and soon fell into a deep sleep. Beads of perspiration bubbled up on his forehead and his breathing became easier.

"The tonic is doing its work," Increase Joseph's father said.

When Increase Joseph awakened the following day, one word formed on his lips, "Mas-sage." His wife thought it was a strange request, but she quickly began rubbing Increase Joseph's back and neck. As his wife worked on his feverish body, he kept mumbling, "mas-sage, mas-sage."

"I'm doing my best," she said as she worked harder.

For three days Increase Joseph would sleep deeply, sweat profusely, and then jerk awake muttering "mas-sage," "mas-sage." Increase Joseph's father and mother took turns rubbing his back and as they did, he constantly babbled only the word, "mas-sage, mas-sage."

"That boy is touched in the head," his mother said on the third day. "We're doing the best job we know to massage him, and all he does is call for more."

On the fourth day, he awakened and repeated the word, except this time he was clearer. "Message," he said. "I've received a message. A message from God."

"You don't want another massage?" Elwina asked.

"I've never wanted a massage," he blurted out. "I hate massages. I have a message from on high. Word from the highest authority. I must rise up. I must rise up and speak." And so he did.

Chapter 3
Preaching

Plum Falls, New York
July 1850

Increase Joseph's recovery was nothing less than miraculous. Not only did his ability to speak return, but his voice was now deeper and more powerful. Words seemed to flow off his lips like melt water from a spring thaw. Before his near fatal accident, he seldom spoke, now he never stopped. He gave orations to the horses as they worked the fields. He talked to the cows when he milked them. He spoke to the chickens when he gathered eggs. All of this was practice of course, for he knew he had been called to speak for a new religion. He was gathering the words, sorting out the ideas, arranging his thoughts as he spoke to the critters around the farm. He seldom mentioned his newly acquired gift to his parents, or even to his wife for fear they would not understand. He worried some that they might think the lightning affected his mind, seared some place where old traditions were stored, and long-standing beliefs were held. But he realized he already had these ideas before the lightning strike. Lightning gave him a new voice and a resolve to stand up and speak out. In some mysterious way, the combination of the tonic and the lightning gave him the tools to express himself beyond anything he thought possible.

He was building up courage to step into the bandstand in the village square at Plum Falls and begin his pilgrimage, to begin his crusade for a new way of thinking about God. He pulled on a pair of long black pants, slipped into a tattered black coat, and put on a wide-brimmed black hat that was his grandfather's. But something was missing. He had watched preachers, many of them. Each carried a Bible, which they waved when they spoke. He didn't want to wave a Bible. But he needed something. Something that looked theological. Something that would add religious authority to his appearance. In the back of a drawer in the bureau that stood in the dining room of their sparsely furnished farm home, he found a red book — owned by one of his ancestors. It was just the right size to fit in his back pocket.

He told his wife that he was headed for Plum Falls for a couple hours and would be back shortly. He kissed his baby son on the cheek and he was off, walking confidently along the narrow road, his head high and his arms swinging.

People in Plum Falls knew about his tragic accident, and how his hair had turned white. As he walked down Main Street, dodging the occasional horse and carriage, folks stared at him in wonder. Everyone knew of lightning that killed many cows and horses over the years, and farmers, too. Here was a survivor, walking down Main Street with no apparent injuries, except for a head of white hair that touched his shoulders and contrasted with his black hat and black coat. People stepped aside as he passed; a few spoke, said "Howdy," but nothing more. They were mostly amazed to see him alive, even if he looked quite different than they remembered.

Increase Joseph climbed the steps to the bandstand and looked out into the park. The sun had just set on this warm summer evening. Children were playing, chasing each other, laughing. A few women gathered on the park benches to rest or to wait while husbands visited the local saloon. A handful of men sat talking in one corner of the park while their wives shopped for groceries at the general store. In the distance, a dog barked.

People in the park didn't seem to notice this figure in black standing in the bandstand, peering out from under a black hat.

"Sisters and brothers," Increase Joseph intoned. One of the mothers sitting closest to the bandstand looked around for her little boy who was playing in the sand nearby. "Come here, Johnny," she said.

"I stand before you on this beautiful evening to bring you a word from God."

The woman with the little boy quickly got up from her bench, gathered up her packages, took the boy by the hand and hurried away.

Increase Joseph continued. "We are destroying our land. How you ask? We are destroying our land by allowing the waters from heaven to wash it away. We are destroying our land by letting the winds blow it away. We are destroying our land by growing crops where no crops should be grown."

A few more people got up and left the park,

dragging their protesting children with them. But three rough looking fellows from the cluster of men in the corner moved closer to the bandstand.

"We have forgotten that we are from the land, and to the land we will return. It is the land that nourishes us and gives us life."

"What's that you say?" one of the young men who moved closer asked.

"We must learn to love the land as we love God, ourselves and our neighbors," Increase Joseph said in a voice that carried well beyond the park.

"You a preacher? Aren't you the one who was struck by lighting? Aren't you a farmer?" the young man asked with a quizzical look on his face.

"I am a preacher," Increase Joseph said confidently.

"Where's your Bible?"

"I have no Bible."

"How can you preach without a Bible?"

"My words come directly from God."

"What's that red book in your hand?"

Increase Joseph hesitated for a moment. He didn't expect anyone to ask him about the Red Book that he had been waving as he spoke.

"It's a red book." Increase Joseph answered.

"Well, I can see that. What's in that red book?"

"Important words of belief," Increase Joseph said.

"Why don't you read from it? We'd like to hear what it says. Wouldn't we boys?" The young man turned to his friends who were shaking their heads up and down and starting to laugh as they enjoyed the exchange.

Increase Joseph opened the red book to page one.

"The land comes first," he said. He repeated it, "The land comes first." His voice was loud, deep and confident.

"Don't sound like no religious belief to me," the young heckler said. "Don't sound like much of anything. How come you're standin' up their spoutin' off about dirt?"

"It's the land, young man. I'm talking about the land and how we must take care of it or we shall all perish."

"You're a crazy man," the heckler said as he and his friends walked away, laughing about what they just heard.

Increase Joseph went on speaking although there was not one person in the park. A stray dog, a brown skinny creature, sat on its haunches, and looked up at Increase Joseph, whined now and again, and even at one point stuck its nose up and howled at the moon that was creeping up over the Mercantile store across the street.

Finally, the dog walked up to the bandstand, lifted a hind leg, and then moved off.

Increase Joseph slipped the Red Book in his back pocket, stepped down from the bandstand and started for home. He strode along the country road, the moon lighting his way and reflecting from his long white hair.

Chapter 4
Leaving Home
April 1852

The small group gathered in a field on the Link farm, which was a short distance from Plum Falls. They stood in a ragged circle, men and women and children of various ages. Little patches of snow remained on the hillsides and along the north side of the nearby woodlot, but the bright April sun warmed the group and encouraged them as they prepared for their journey west.

These were the families that had turned out for Increase Joseph Link's Saturday night preaching sessions in the village park. These were the farmers who believed the words he spoke and respected his gumption for saying them. They supported him when many others taunted and even threatened him. After much contemplation and prayer, these were the families who agreed to move with him to the new state of Wisconsin, to begin afresh on soil that had never before seen the plow. They listened intently when Increase Joseph read from the green *Emigrant's Hand Book and Guide to Wisconsin*, which was published in 1851.

"Central Wisconsin," he read "is a region of uniform aspect, beautifully diversified with timber openings and small prairies, which in fertility of soil can scarcely be surpassed; there are but few spots combining all the natural elements of health, wealth, and beauty, in a degree equal to this. The soil is soft, black and rich; the most exhausting processes make no sensible drain upon its richness."

They could hardly believe their ears for the soil of their farms in upper New York State had badly run out and each year seemed to yield fewer crops. Besides the Wisconsin lands being rich and new, they all looked forward to following Increase Joseph's tenets for nurturing the land as they nurtured themselves.

They gathered this Monday morning at the Link farm as final tribute to their birthplace and to request safe journey for the long trip to Wisconsin.

Increase Joseph Link wore his usual black shirt and pants, a long black coat and a black hat that he pulled down to his ears. His flowing white hair stuck out everywhere.

Increase Joseph raised his long arms and looked out over the group of plainly dressed men and women. His wife Elwina and son, Increase Joseph II, now two, stood next to him.

"We are about to embark on a great journey," Increase Joseph Link said. "We are here today to bid farewell to the home of our birth, and to gird ourselves for the challenges of our journey and a new land."

His voice rose in volume and he looked skyward, as if to gather inspiration from the heavens.

"Help us with safe journey. Let the land that

has nurtured us so far continue to do so in a new place. Now let each of us pray in our own way."

Increase Joseph held high the Red Book that had taken on mystical characteristics. People wondered what words it contained. They must be powerful words, as the book was a guide for everything that Increase Joseph said and did.

A great silence settled over the group of New York farmers about to embark on a new adventure. Several of them folded their hands and looked skyward. One couple knelt and bowed their heads. Several, with their hands shoved deep in their pockets, stood staring straight ahead. The children, behaving at first, began to fidget as the silent prayer continued.

A meadowlark called from the pasture field to their right. A black crow flew over; some later claimed it was a symbol — but a symbol for what?

The silent prayer continued. Now even the most devout wanted to get on with it, to load their meager belongings on the steam vessel and sail to Sheboygan, Wisconsin, their first, but not final destination.

Increase Joseph Link stood like a statue clothed in black, his deep set eyes closed and his hands, holding the Red Book, folded in front of him. At first he seemed to be moving his lips, silently. But they too were now stilled. All eyes were on him, waiting, anticipating, hoping that he would say something, that he would declare the prayer over, and that they could begin their long journey.

Emil Groskeep, in his early thirties, tall, muscular and with wide-set eyes stood closest to Increase Joseph. Groskeep heard it first. It was a kind of buzzing sound, with a hint of a whistle. At first

Emil thought it was the morning breeze playing tricks as it moved over the silent, praying group. But now he knew for sure. The sound came from Increase Joseph.

Emil whispered to his wife standing at his side. "I think our spiritual leader is asleep." It was indeed so. Like an old plow horse that could sleep standing up, this great spiritual leader possessed the same capability.

The word was passed along, in quiet whispers, "Increase Joseph is asleep." By the time the message traveled full circle, Emil Groskeep, who began the message, heard "Increase Joseph is a sheep." He smiled, along with all the others who heard the message incorrectly.

Just then, Increase Joseph Link's eyes snapped open. "Amen" he said with a loud clear voice. "Let the journey begin."

The following morning was drizzly and cool. Increase Joseph was up early, making final preparations for the trip. As he stood on the porch of the farmhouse where he was born, facing his mother and father, no words were passed between son and parents. Just as he turned to leave, his father stepped up to his son, thrust a piece of yellowing paper in his pocket and said, "You'll find this handy." Then the senior Link handed his son a small box containing several bottles of tonic.

Increase Joseph joined the other families that called themselves the Standalone Fellowship. On this cool, wet spring morning, they set out from Plum Falls, New York, with wagons and oxen, worn out milk cows, skinny pigs and a few scraggly sheep. They headed for Buffalo, a distance of about twenty miles. The plan was to sell their animals and wagons in Buffalo. With the money they would buy new equipment and farm animals when they arrived in Sheboygan, Wisconsin.

As the caravan moved slowly along the dusty road with Increase Joseph Link, his wife and young son riding in the lead wagon, several of the diverse group of followers wondered if they had made the right decision. Some of the families had lived in New York State from the middle 1700s, before the Revolutionary War. They knew their community; they knew how to farm there. Yet, for their children to have a more promising future, they knew they should move.

Most of the Standalone Fellowship had two major concerns — economic and religious. Each year, as the soil became more depleted on their hilly farms, they grew fewer crops and their skinny animals brought less at market. Most of the group could scarcely make it through the year in New York without having to borrow money from a relative, or they put off buying something that was necessary like replacing an ox that had died.

Members of the group had also grown disenchanted with the community church where they had all been members. The preacher was constantly asking them to contribute more money for its upkeep. The preacher and a few longtime members who would never leave New York made all the decisions such as when services would be held and what hymns would be sung. But worse, this same small clique, with the preacher leading the charge, made it known that everyone who didn't follow the dictates of the church, in every way, from attending services on Sunday morning, to making sure the collection plate was properly filled, was on their way to hell.

"Sinner" became the popular word. People would leave Sunday morning services with that word ringing in their heads. "You were born in sin, you remain in sin." For many people, it soon became clear that they saw no hope in ever seeing a life in the hereafter. They walked to and from church each Sunday, fearful of saying anything that might hurry their trip to hell.

Then Increase Joseph Link came along. Actually he had been there all the while, having been born and raised in the community, but different from others, he went off to college to become a preacher. With few exceptions, everyone else in the group that walked the road to Buffalo that dreary April morning had little more than a rudimentary education, although all the adults knew how to read and write.

Some in the group had questions about Increase Joseph Link, this preacher man with a mane of white hair who always dressed in black. He was never seen without his Red Book. When Increase Joseph wasn't doing something else, he had his nose in that Red Book, studying it carefully. He could be profound and many thought prophetic as he talked about this new religion where each person could believe as he or she wished, that relationship and love replaced "sinner," and people, the land, and God formed a triune foundation.

But Increase Joseph Link had another side, an eccentric, unpredictable side that worried some people and gave others a chuckle like when he fell asleep during the long prayer yesterday in Link's pasture. The Standalone Fellowship followed him because they liked what he said and the way he said it — even though their understanding of his message varied considerably.

A few farmers, the Judd brothers for example, decided on the trip because they knew their farms were failing and they needed to start afresh. They weren't much for religion, no matter how it was dished up. Others followed because of the religion. Increase Joseph's message seemed to give them more leeway, more opportunity to express themselves in their own way.

The local pastor was increasingly provoked by Increase Joseph's outdoor preaching. One of the local pastor's sermons a few Sundays ago was titled "The Devil's Messenger," a scathing account disguised but clearly pointed at Increase Joseph.

Henry and Abigail Bakken with their two year old daughter, Henrietta, were non-farmers in the group. Henry and Abigail, like Increase Joseph, had more than a basic education. Henry had a full red beard, was short, round faced and wore wire-rimmed glasses. He worked at the *Plum Falls Reporter* and gotten himself in trouble by writing negative stories about the local church. A recent editorial he wrote was titled, "Home Preacher goes too far stating that sin is everywhere with no hope for anyone." Henry and his wife planned to start a newspaper in Wisconsin. Increase Joseph's religion sounded a little unusual to them, but they, like others, had come to respect the sincerity of the man in black and had joined the Standalone Fellowship.

A few people were simply along for the ride. They wanted a new adventure, to see a new place, to do something different. Joe and John Judd, bachelor farmer brothers who neither attended

church nor cared much about farming, other than
it was all they knew how to do, fell into this cat-
egory. They were young, strong, liked a good time,
and besides, they might find brides in Wisconsin
so they could give up cooking and housekeeping,
not that they spent much time doing either. Joe
was the tall brother, with hair as black as night
and as coarse as a horse's tail, muscular arms that
reflected years of hard work, and a face that seldom smiled. John, shorter but equally muscular
with thinning brown hair, a face that smiled easy
and a voice that laughed often.

The caravan of thirty some people, the women
and young children riding in the wagons with
trunks, tables, chairs, stoves, and other belongings and the men and older children walking,
slowly made their way toward Buffalo. The oxen
plodded along, setting the pace for the group. Pigs
and sheep and red Durham milk cows strayed often and had to be herded back onto the road. Road
dust accumulated on everything and everyone.
The quiet of the morning was disrupted by the occasional crack of a bull whip over the backs of a
reluctant oxen team, and the yells at farm animals
that walked everywhere but on the road.

A couple of the women were crying, the dust
smearing their tears. They were thinking of their
families that they were leaving behind and may
never see again — parents, brothers and sisters.
Men walked without expression, each thinking his
own thoughts, each revealing little in facial expression.

After several hours of walking they saw Buffalo
in the distance. It was a teeming lake port town,
especially since steam vessels had become a popu-

lar form of transportation on the Great Lakes. They could hear the steamboat whistles of boats coming and going — a sound at the same time eerie and foreboding, yet a sound of promise and new beginnings. Now even the animals seemed to catch some of the excitement of the journey and needed little encouragement.

Increase Joseph signaled the group to stop. He stood up on the back of his wagon, his ever-present Red Book in his hand. He held up both hands and looked skyward.

"Lo, we have reached Buffalo," he said in a voice loud and clear. Of course this was a fact that didn't need to be announced as everyone could see what Increase Joseph saw.

Increase Joseph turned, stepped down from the wagon, fished in his pocket for a bottle of tonic. He took a long drink of the elixir and then prodded his team of oxen to continue. Several people in the group shook their heads. They wondered what he was drinking. They were mostly but not quite sure that it wasn't liquor because Increase Joseph spoke often about the evils of strong drink.

"Strange fellow," Joe Judd said.

"Yup," his brother John said as he encouraged his oxen to start moving.

Chapter 5
Buffalo

The caravan stopped just outside Buffalo and set up camp in a farmer's field. Increase Joseph had gotten permission from the farmer. He insisted the group place the wagons in a circle. "In case there might be some difficulty during the night." He also appointed night guards to patrol the perimeter of their camp until dawn.

"You'd think we were traveling in Indian country," one of the men said under his breath, but everyone did as their spiritual leader instructed.

When the travelers were settled, several campfires could be spotted as women prepared the evening meal. Increase Joseph and Henry Bakken, the newspaperman, walked the short distance into Buffalo in search of a buyer for their meager possessions. It was nearly dark when they returned with two roughly dressed men driving a team and wagon. One was short and thin; the other tall with an ample belly. Both looked, and smelled like they hadn't had a bath in weeks.

"Look around," Increase Joseph said. "These are prize animals, every one of them. And check these wagons, only the best they are."

Everyone in the group knew none of this was true. The animals were skinny and undernourished. The oxen were old and tired from years of plowing. The wagons were worn out. Wagon boxes had broken boards; nearly every one had at least one wheel that needed repair.

"Not much here," the tall rough dressed man said as he spat tobacco juice on the ground in front of Increase Joseph. Increase Joseph jumped back as the some of the brown juice splattered on his pant leg.

No one said anything for a time. A cow bawled for her calf. "Little Sidney, where you gone to," one of the women in the group called as she searched for her son.

"Sit here by my fire and share a cup of coffee with us," Increase Joseph said. Elwina Link, Joseph's wife, in the background but always present, quickly found coffee cups for the tough looking pair and the negotiating team.

"Thank you ma'am," the short man said.

"How about a fresh baked cookie?" Elwina asked.

"Don't mind if I do," the tall man with the chaw of tobacco answered.

No mention was made of a price for the livestock and equipment.

Increase Joseph excused himself as he walked to his wagon and returned with two large bottles of tonic. He handed a bottle to each of the men.

"What you got here, preacher?"

"This is a famous tonic that's been passed from generation to generation in my family. It cures, it soothes, it restores, and it strengthens. Want to try it?"

"Why not?" the tall man said.

Each man soon drained his bottle of tonic.

"Feeling a might dizzy," the little man said as he tried to stand.

"Tonic's working," Increase Joseph said. "Moving right to the core of your being."

"Whas in that stuff, sagotta real kick to it," the tall man said, his words slurred.

"What'd you say you'd offer for all this?" Increase Joseph said as he waved his arm over the mostly sleeping camp. The number was nearly twice what he expected.

"An we'll pay you right now," the little man said. He had great difficulty spitting out the words. "Before there be any mind changin'." He weaved back and forth in front of the dying fire. With some challenge he fished several coins out of his pocket, counting them in the dim light of the embers.

"We'll deliver everything to your livery stable first thing in the morning," Increase Joseph said as they shook hands all around.

"Before you go, we must offer a prayer," Increase Joseph said. The two men from town didn't look like the praying kind, but they stood, removed their hats, bowed their heads, and swayed back and forth trying to keep their balance.

"Thank you Lord," Increase Joseph began. "For these two generous men from Buffalo. For their willingness to buy our few possessions so we can continue our journey. For their willingness to hear our plans and share our story. For their intelligence and great bargaining skills."

"Amen," broke in Henry Bakken. Bakken thought if this prayer was to go on, as it seemed likely to, Increase Joseph would make these conniving crooks into saints. Or worse, they would change their minds about the bad deal that they just struck.

"Amen," said Increase Joseph. He shook his head as if returning from some unknown place.

"Safe . . . journey . . . to you . . . Preacher Rink," said the man with the cud of tobacco still resting in his cheek. The words came slowly..

The wagon with the two men creaked off toward town. The tall man was stretched out in the back on the rough boards, the short man sat slumped over on the driving seat.

Henry Bakken slapped Increase Joseph on the back. A small cloud of dust rose from his black coat.

"You sure pulled one over on those guys. Yes, you did," Bakken said.

"It's the Lord's doing," Increase Joseph said, not smiling.

"Yeah, sure," said Bakken as everyone settled down for a night of rest.

The next morning the group ate breakfast and traveled the short distance to Buffalo where they delivered their livestock, wagons, and other implements to the livery stable. The two men they dealt with the previous night were nowhere in sight. Then they headed for the office of the steamship line where Increase Joseph booked passage on the steamship *Queen of the Lakes* that was scheduled to leave Buffalo at 6:00 p.m.

The "Queen" held 110 passengers with a crew of thirty. Increase Joseph bought everyone's tickets — $3.00 each in steerage (no meals and no sleeping accommodations). Increase Joseph booked a cabin for himself and his wife for $8.00

each, their baby was free. Their meals would be provided, they had comfortable sleeping accommodations, and the "privileges of the boat," the sign at the ticket office said.

During the day, the group explored the dock area, watching several steamships load and unload. A steady stream of horse drawn wagons arrived at the docks, carrying wood for the steamships' boilers.

At 4:30 p.m. the Standalone Fellowship walked up the gangplank and onto the deck of the "Queen of The Lakes." Workmen, drenched in sweat from carting load after load of wood onto the ship, pushed by them.

When everyone boarded and all of the trunks, stoves, furniture, and other small farming equipment were loaded, everyone gathered on deck for an anticipated prayer meeting.

But there was no prayer. Later, the group learned that Increase Joseph was earlier seen standing at the edge of the dock hunched over. The mere sight of the ship made him seasick. No one on board saw Increase Joseph until they passed Detroit, and then they saw him leaning over the rail. He was apparently sick the entire trip even though the waters of Lakes Erie, Huron, and Michigan were not especially rough.

On the morning of the third day of their trip the "Queen of the Lakes" passed through the straits of Mackinac and entered Lake Michigan. People lined the rails of the steamship where they could soon watch the densely wooded shoreline of Wisconsin. As they steamed along, they spotted an occasional stump-filled clearing with a log cabin in its center and a small log barn near the dense forest. At one farmstead, children played in the yard and waved at the steamship that plowed its way south.

The following morning, when the group awakened, the scene changed little. Soon they approached Manitowoc, a village of about 600 people, the steamship captain said, with several log cabins, business places, and a yet not well-developed harbor.

At noon on the fourth day, the "Queen of the Lakes" slowly eased up to the pier in Sheboygan. Other steamships were tied nearby, loading and unloading. For those first seeing the scene it was one of utter confusion. Teamsters were yelling at their horses. Workmen were toting kitchen stoves, furniture, plows, and trunks of various sizes and descriptions from the ships to the docks.

When everyone in the Standalone Fellowship had disembarked, they gathered on shore, awaiting word from their leader, Increase Joseph. With his Red Book in hand, he climbed onto a trunk, with a little help, as he hadn't yet recovered from his seasickness.

In a voice less strong than normal, Increase Joseph, whose face was as white as his hair said, "We have reached She-boygan." The words were scarcely uttered when he quickly brought his hand to his mouth, stumbled down from the trunk and staggered to the water's edge. He frantically searched for his bottle of tonic that he apparently left in his cabin on the boat.

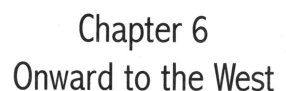

Chapter 6
Onward to the West

Sheboygan, Wisconsin
April 1852

Fortified by the tonic, Increase Joseph quickly gained his land legs. He and Henry Bakken were off visiting the livestock and farm machinery dealers in Sheboygan, buying oxen, milk cows, wagons, and plows. Once people learned where they were traveling, several mentioned stopping at Wade House.

Soon the caravan's eight teams of oxen, eight wagons, twelve cows, and assorted farm machinery were on the plank road from Sheboygan to Fond du Lac. Their goal for the first night was Greenbush, where Sylvanus Wade and his wife Betsy just the year before opened Wade House, an inn where the families with small children could rest under a roof, and where all could enjoy Betsy Wade's fine cooking.

The distance to Greenbush from Sheboygan was only 22 miles, yet it was almost dark before the tired group pulled onto the Wade House grounds. Although the plank road was an obvious improvement from walking through the mud caused by the recent rains, the rough sawed planks sometimes shifted and caused an ox's foot to slip between them. And in the lowest places along the road, water oozed up between the cracks in the planks making the wood slippery and travel difficult for the usually sure footed oxen.

"Hal-lo," said Sylvanus Wade when Increase Joseph stopped his team in front of the inn. "Where you folks from?" Wade inquired.

"We come from Plum Falls, New York State," replied Increase Joseph.

"You look like a preacher man," said Wade.

"I am a preacher," said Increase Joseph. "These are my flock. We are the Standalone Fellowship and we are on our way in search of new land and a new life."

"That right?" said Wade.

"Right it is. We are seekers of the truth, searchers for the right way, pilgrims on the road to a new beginning."

"Well come on in," beckoned Sylvanus Wade. "All are welcome in our inn, no matter what their purpose or destination."

Soon everyone, all thirty-two members of the Fellowship, was seated around long tables in the inn. Steaming platters of potatoes and roast beef stood in front of them.

"Let's bow our heads," Increase Joseph commanded.

"Great God on high, we thank you for our safe journey across the rough waters from Buffalo to Sheboygan." He pronounced it "she-a-boy-a-gan." "We thank you for safe journey along the rough and slippery trail leading to this fine inn. We thank these fine people, Sylvanus and Betsy Wade for

constructing this wonderful building and for serving tired travelers as they wind their way west, on
their search for new beginnings."

The children began to fidget. The less religious
in the group saw the mounds of delicious home-
cooked food getting cold. Even the believers began to look toward Increase Joseph, who stood
behind his chair with his eyes closed and the Red
Book raised high above his head.

"We are privileged as pilgrims on the trail of life.
So privileged to live at this time and be in this place.
So privileged. So privileged." Increase Joseph's
thoughts appeared stuck on a single topic. He took
a deep breath, waved the Red Book in a big circle
and continued. "So privileged."

Someone in the group said, in a loud voice,
"Amen." Increase Joseph's eyes snapped open.
He immediately sat down in his chair at the end of
the table and said, "Pass the potatoes."

Mr. Wade joined them as they ate, sharing a little
of the history of the area and answering questions.

"Will the Indians attack us?" young Joey
Trutweiller asked.

"Might see some Menominee Indians, but
they're friendly and just as curious to look at you
as you are them," Mr. Wade answered.

"How's the trail to Fond du Lac?" Henry Bakken
inquired.

"About the same as the one to Sheboygan, a
plank road. Ground's a little higher though, planks
probably won't be as slippery."

The younger children were ready for bed, and
soon everyone was turned in, ready to start out
fresh in the morning.

At first light, with yokes in place, the oxen and

their heavily loaded wagons set out once more on the plank road toward Fond du Lac a distance of some thirty miles from Greenbush. Everyone waved to the Wades, who stood in front of their fine inn. "Good luck to you all," Sylvanus Wade shouted as the Standalone Fellowship and its string of heavy wagons lumbered along the trail.

The day was uneventful and by late afternoon the party reached the huge hill that overlooked the bustling city of Fond du Lac and Lake Winnebago that disappeared into the mists to the north.

"What a sight it is," said Increase Joseph. "The Lord has truly blessed this country."

No one disagreed, as everyone stood and gazed at a wooded countryside, the beautiful blue lake and the bustle of a thriving city. They heard the mill saw with its steam-powered blade slicing through great native white pines and forming two by fours, and one-by-twelves, and heavy timbers for building churches and barns and school houses. They saw horses and wagons everywhere, hauling lumber, toting wheat and flour, carrying windows and doors for building new homes.

Slowly the caravan of ox drawn wagons moved down the hill and into the city. The smells of commerce hung heavy in the air — fresh cut wood, horse sweat, manure strewn rutted streets. And the sounds, too. Dray drivers shouting at their teams. Dogs barking.

A heavy set whiskered driver with an overloaded wagon and a straining team of black horses approached the procession. The driver was cursing his team, shouting profanities to the top of his voice. When he came alongside Increase Joseph's wagon, Increase Joseph said in his deep voice, "Such language is neither necessary nor appropriate."

"What, what?" the surprised wagon driver said.

"You are demeaning the Lord with such language and injuring the ears of the young ones who ride in these wagons."

"Go to hell," the man said as he snapped the reins over the backs of the straining team. Increase Joseph did not reply, but urged on his oxen team.

Soon the Standalone Fellowship with its tired oxen and even more tired members reached an open field with a log cabin at the end of it. Increase Joseph asked permission at the cabin, and the group once more circled their wagons in the little field before cooking their evening meal over smoky campfires. Several commented on how they wished the Wade House were located on this side of Fond du Lac. Increase Joseph inquired about the distance to Berlin, the trading post on the Fox River. They expected to spend the next night there on the way to the government lands beyond Willow River.

Chapter 7
Naming The Lake

Link Lake, Wisconsin
May 1852

When he and his followers arrived in Ames County, Wisconsin, Increase Joseph Link had his choice of where they might settle. A vast new area opened after the 1848 Indian Treaty at Lake Poygan. The area he selected was blessed with rolling fertile soil, a nearby lake and many naturally growing white pine trees. Link himself chose 160 acres on the south end of a long narrow lake that teemed with fish and provided nesting sites for scores of wild ducks and other wildlife.

Not long after the families arrived and constructed cabins from the logs harvested in the great forest of white pines north of the lake, they all gathered at Increase Joseph's farm on a warm Sunday afternoon. Everyone thought the afternoon was to be one of special celebration and thanksgiving. God looked down on the fellowship with favor. Not one person died on the long trip. Two babies had already been born. And no one was injured seriously in the cabin building, although Adolph Lang chopped off the end of one of his fingers when his ax slipped, and Frederick Henke still walked hunched over after a tree limb snapped back and struck him square in the privates.

The men, women, and children gathered on the shores of this pristine body of water and watched as their spiritual leader waded out into the water fully clothed, complete with black hat. In one hand he carried the Red Book, the guidebook for the fellowship. In the other hand he carried a three-tined pitchfork.

Increase Joseph Link was known for doing things that bordered on the strange. But no one said anything. After all, he was their spiritual leader and he had shown them the way from New York State to this new place. A warm spring breeze blew from the south, rippling the clear blue lake. Bird song was everywhere, robins, redwing blackbirds. Even quail were whistling, "bob white, bob white," and a wild turkey gobbled far off in the woods, its call drifting over the water.

Slowly, Increase Joseph waded into ever-deeper water. When he was waist deep he turned and faced the group assembled on shore.

"We are here for an auspicious reason," he said in his deep, spiritual voice that rolled over the water like God's very utterances.

"What does 'auspicious' mean?" Andrew Blackwell, a thin, serious man whispered to his wife, Mabel.

"Shh!" she said. "We'll soon find out."

Increase Joseph lifted the Red Book high over his head and looked up. Even the bird song quelled during this moment of spiritual intensity. Children ceased fidgeting as they watched this great spiritual leader look to the heavens for inspiration and thanksgiving.

Once more Increase Joseph began speaking. "We are gathered here today," he intoned. "We are gathered here today." He lifted the pitchfork out of the water and slammed it down into the bottom of the lake with a mighty thrust. As he did so he said in a loud voice, "This body of water shall forever from this day forward be known as Link Lake."

As the words "Link Lake" flowed out of his mouth, Increase Joseph sank from view. In an instant there was nothing to be seen except a little circle of water into which he disappeared and a black hat that began floating toward shore.

There was stunned disbelief. Two young men of the fellowship plunged into the water, grabbed Increase Joseph and dragged him to shore sputtering and spitting. "Big hole out there," he said between coughs. "Big hole."

With the lake named, the cabins and barns built, and crops planted, the Fellowship members commenced building their church. Increase Joseph provided the land for the church building, just up the trail from his cabin and atop a little hill that commanded a view of Link Lake.

Before the building was completed, the Fellowship gathered on the church hill every Sunday afternoon to worship. They agreed, one of the few things for which there was total accord, that no services should be conducted on Sunday mornings. It made no sense to disrupt a fine night's sleep by crawling out of bed on an early Sunday morning to attend church. All services would be held on Sunday afternoons.

At the beginning of each service, Increase Joseph held up his arms and waved his hands to motion silence. A kind of spiritual silence would settle over the group. As was the style of the Standalone Fellowship, Increase Joseph provided an hour of spellbinding oratory, waving the Red Book like a kind of spiritual flag the entire time. (The Red Book looked a bit tattered after its immersion in Link Lake.)

If someone else had something to say, that person, man or woman, would stand up and say it. Increase Joseph, when asked about this practice by an outsider, answered, "When God has something he wants someone to say, He'll put the words in the person's mouth."

Sometimes there was a question about the motivation for the comments presented, and some debate as to whether God was really the source for the words. For instance, on a muggy Sunday afternoon, while the Fellowship members were still meeting out in the open, Jacob Ornsby stood up, brushed back his long black stringy hair and began a long discourse about the inconvenience of mosquitoes. As if speaking for God himself, Jacob began, "Of all my creations, large and small, strong and meek, beautiful and ordinary, I made one major blunder. That blunder was the creation of the blood sucking, miserable, irritating, annoying, loud buzzing, itch-creating mosquito. For this I am sorry and hope all my subjects will excuse the error of my ways and my over-zealousness in creating creatures without more thought of their actions."

The Fellowship listened attentively, but silently. Several wondered if God was one to apologize for an apparent indiscretion. Jacob seemed to believe that God put these words in his mouth, and he had every right to speak them for this was the way of the Standalone Fellowship, each person was entitled to his beliefs and the way in which he wanted to express them.

Building the church became a challenge because Increase Joseph insisted that the building be round.

"There is no place to hide in a round building," Increase Joseph said. Logs, no matter how much they were encouraged, did not lend themselves to circular construction. Although building a round church was their goal, the building in reality had 16 sides. From a distance it appeared round, but up close one could see the great effort the Fellowship members took to lift into place carefully cut and notched logs, none longer than six feet. Floor to ceiling clear windows were placed on the side of the church overlooking Link Lake. Just outside the windows, a little to the side, stood a clump of old, scraggly jack pine trees.

Finally, on a Sunday in late August, the church was ready for services. No longer did the Fellowship have to meet in the field with the hot sun pouring down on them, and swarms of mosquitoes and black flies tearing at their hides. No longer did Increase Joseph have to compete with the wind and the sound of birds when he delivered his message of clear thought and freedom, and the power of standing alone together as they celebrated the relationship of God, people, and the land.

The seats in the church, rough sawed oak

planks, had no backs or other attempts at personal comfort. "The Word more freely enters the mind if the seat is uncomfortable," was Increase Joseph's answer to those who inquired about putting backs on the seats. The church was arranged with the seats circling a pit formed of fieldstone in the exact center of the structure. Three stone steps led down to the preaching pit, as it came to be called. There was no pulpit, podium, or other contrivance to separate speaker from audience, only a small handmade wooden table.

"Anyone who speaks to the Fellowship should not stand above them, for it is a humbling experience and one of honor to speak to others," Increase Joseph said. The many times they met outside, the Fellowship always was placed on the upside of a hill, with Increase Joseph standing at the bottom.

On that warm Sunday afternoon, the Fellowship, most of whom helped to build the church, began filing into the structure for the first service. The fresh smell of sawdust on the floor and the aroma of newly placed pine logs filled the air. It was clearly a day of celebration and a new step in the progress of the Fellowship that only a few short months ago lived in New York State.

With everyone seated, Increase Joseph, attired in black from head to foot, strode through the open door, along the aisle that led to the stone pit. Before entering the building, he took a long deep drink of the tonic; a practice that he claimed calmed his nerves and sharpened his thoughts. In place at the bottom of the pit, he stood with his head bowed and his hands at his side. The muffled sound of a crow could be heard through the open window, and a slight breeze off the lake gently caressed the windblown jack pine trees. Otherwise the room with filled with a deep spiritual quiet.

Finally, Increase Joseph, his long white hair carefully combed, lifted the tattered Red Book high over his head.

"Brothers and sisters," he intoned. His voice, the same one he used when speaking outside, bounced off the walls of the new building. Immediately, three babies began wailing. Someone later reported that Increase Joseph's voice reminded them of being in the center of an immense rainstorm, with ear-splitting claps of thunder repeating again and again. Others compared his voice to sticking your head in an empty rain barrel while someone dropped in a lighted firecracker.

"Brothers and sisters," Increase Joseph roared again. More babies began crying. "This is a day for all of us to remember forever. We are gathered here in God's house to celebrate his work."

"Amen," someone said from the back row.

"Hallelujah is the word brother. This is a day for praise and joy," Increase Joseph said.

"Hallelujah!" several people spoke in unison.

"I had a dream last night," Increase Joseph said. "I dreamed of a time when everyone was free to think and speak their own thoughts without criticism or condemnation. I dreamed of a time when everyone was no longer shackled by ancient doctrine, never changing writings, and time worn traditions."

"Hallelujah!" a little man with a long black beard said. "Hallelujah!"

Increase Joseph raised the Red Book high over his head. People knew that when their spiritual leader did this, he was saying something important.

"I had a dream," Increase Joseph intoned, "Of a time when people cared for the land as the land cared for them. A time when people took care of each other as God takes care of each of us. A time when all God's creatures, the birds and the animals, the trees and the wild flowers, the air we breathe and the water we drink, the very soil we walk on became one with us."

Increase Joseph stopped speaking and put his hands to his sides. He once more bowed his head and closed his eyes. Everyone in the audience had their eyes on him, not knowing what was coming next.

"Hallelujah!" the bearded man said finally, breaking the silence.

Increase Joseph lifted the top from a small wooden box that stood unnoticed beside him. He placed the Red Book on the little wooden table that stood next to him, and thrust both hands into the box, filling them with a granular material. He lifted his hands over his head, bits of brown material dribbling from around his fingers and sifting to the floor.

"What have I got here?" Increase Joseph asked. "What have I got in my hands?" The words careened off the log walls and seem to gather somewhere under the ceiling before spilling out over the audience as the granular material was spilling over the floor.

A little boy near the front of the church said in a quiet, quizzical voice, "Dirt?"

"Not dirt. Not dirt. This is land, the land that is the mother of us all."

The little boy turned to his mother and whispered, "Looks like dirt to me, Ma,"

"Shh!" his mother said, smiling.

"We are all part of the land, have been and forever will be. As farmers it is our God given task to care for the land, to till it, nourish it, protect it and above all give it respect. In return the land will feed us, embrace us and give us the joy that comes with bountiful harvest."

Brown soil continued sifting from Increase Joseph's hands as he talked; some of it spilled down the front of his black coat.

"It is our connection to the land that nourishes our souls, that gives us a glimpse into God's wonderful creation."

As Increase Joseph talked, he became more excited. Perspiration beaded on his forehead. His hands, now free of soil, began to tremble.

"I had a dream. I had a dream . . ." Increase Joseph's voice trailed off as he stopped speaking, picked up the Red Book and stood with his hands by his sides and his head bowed. Then he slumped down on one of the nearby benches.

"Amen," someone from the back said.

Henry Bakken, Increase Joseph's long time friend rushed to him.

"Are you all right, Increase Joseph?"

The man in black shook his head and his eyes snapped open.

"Huh?"

"Are you feeling all right, Increase Joseph?"

The spiritual leader was looking at his hands. "Where'd this dirt come from? How'd this dirt get on my hands, and my coat? Who brought this dirt into the church?"

Chapter 8
Village of Link Lake
August 1852

The newly founded Village of Link Lake straddled a fast moving trout stream that flowed out of the south end of the lake by the same name, on its way toward Lake Winnebago, the Fox River, and eventually Green Bay. While the Fellowship members had earlier been busy building cabins and clearing land, Amos Trutweiller, who was built like a burr oak tree and had been a miller in New York State, worked with his five sturdy sons to build a flour and saw mill near the rapids where Link Creek flowed out of Link Lake. Other businesses sprang up in Link Lake — a mercantile store, wagon making shop, barbershop, livery stable and blacksmith shop, a combination furniture store and undertaker, and the office for the *Link Lake Gazette.* The Standalone Fellowship church stood on top of a little hill, overlooking the village and not far from the Link Lake one-room schoolhouse.

Because the Standalone Fellowship was violently opposed to strong drink, no tavern was allowed in the village, or anywhere in the countryside within ten miles of the village of Link Lake. Tale is told of the German, Adolph Smidmaier who opened the livery stable and blacksmith shop. He had a ruddy red face, a prominent nose and milky eyes. He was not a member of the Fellowship, but was encouraged to settle because he owned several horses and knew how to shoe and care for them.

Smidmaier soon discovered that to buy a glass of beer he must travel to Willow River, some fifteen miles south. Smidmaier knew about the Fellowship's disdain for the amber drink, but he thought he might be able to start a tavern in town, if he named the place something else. So in the vacant lot next to the livery he constructed a little building that he called, "Smidmaier's Sweets Emporium." He would offer a variety of candies, but he would also sell beer — he called it barley water.

Smidmaier's building was completed quickly, thanks to the cooperation of Amos Trutweiller at the mill who sawed out just what Smidmaier requested without delay. Smidmaier was even able to enlist some of the Fellowship's farm boys with the construction.

Smidmaier invited everyone in the community, Standalone members included, for a gala opening at which time he offered free candy and barley water. He offered a special invitation to Increase Joseph and Elwina. Soon everyone was gathered around the barley water tap — none of the group had ever tasted barely water before — and proclaimed what a wonderful drink it was. A couple of men said under their breath that it tasted like beer. Someone suggested a song might be in order. The entire group, young and old alike burst into song, singing the songs that had become a part of the Standalone Fellowship's Sunday services. They especially enjoyed singing what was fast becoming the theme song of the Fellowship, "We Are Alone Together."

> *We are alone together,*
> *Of God and the land*
> *Yet together we stand*
> *As alone we are too.*
> *Simple yet not*
> *A direction but no.*
> *We stand for the land*
> *May it always be so.*

The singing and merriment went on into the night as everyone continued to have a good time drinking Smidmaier's barley water. Adolph Smidmaier thought he had succeeded in his great deception until the next day when Increase Joseph Link tied his horse outside the candy store and walked slowly inside, holding his head. He carried the Red Book in his hand. Without saying a word, he walked up to Adolph Smidmaier and began shaking the Red Book in his face.

Increase Joseph's eyes were bloodshot, and he looked like he had slept in his clothes.

"Do you know what this is?"

"No, I don't think I've seen that little book before."

"Well, this book guides the Standalone Fellowship," Increase Joseph said.

"Yah," Smidmaier said. He had no idea where the conversation was headed, but he had talked with Increase Joseph before and he wasn't always coherent.

"This book is clear. As clear as the water in Link Lake."

"Yah." Smidmaier was thinking that at times the water in Link Lake was a little on the cloudy order, but he didn't mention that.

"The Standalone Fellowship believes that liquor is the devil's brew."

"Yah," said Smidmaier. He wanted to point out that what he was serving was beer and not liquor, but figured this might not be a good time to explain the differences between the two.

"Our people are all sick today," Increase Joseph said. "Some are throwing up, some are sleeping the sleep of death; nobody can work. The women who did not drink your barley water are doing all the chores, chopping wood and forking manure."

"Yah," Smidmaier said. He couldn't suppress a little smile

"I will forbid any of the Fellowship to ever enter this building again," Increase Joseph thundered and immediately wished he hadn't yelled because it only caused his aching head to throb more fiercely.

So that was the end of Smidmaier's Sweets Emporium. He turned the building into an annex for his stable with the hope that one day the Fellowship would change its mind about barley water. They never did.

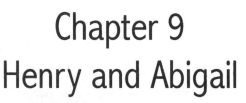

Chapter 9
Henry and Abigail

Henry Bakken and his wife ran the newly organized *Link Lake Gazette*. Bakken, with his neatly trimmed red beard and an ever present striped vest, was easily identified in the growing village of Link Lake located on the far south end of the lake.

Bakken's wife, Abigail, spent much of her time in the newspaper office. She was a short, thin woman, who wore her blond hair in braids and had a most pleasant way about her. She was in charge of selling advertising for the newspaper, a task that she did well. About once a week she made the rounds of the new businesses in Link Lake trying to convince them that it was important to advertise. She even managed to pry a small ad out of Increase Joseph, who used the space to announce the title for the coming week's sermon.

Henry and Abigail's daughter, Henrietta, was the same age as Increase Joseph's son, and the two children often played together. The Bakkens were not only members of the Standalone Fellowship, but they considered Increase Joseph and Elwina friends. When Increase Joseph was severely criticized by church people back in Plum Falls, New York, Henry Bakken stood up for him, and never once wrote anything critical about him in the newspaper.

Even though his support for Increase Joseph was unwavering, he often didn't understand the spiritual leader. Occasionally Bakken wondered if the lightning had indeed seared Increase Joseph's brain. And some days he wondered if Increase Joseph simply liked to hear himself talk, period. Sometimes Increase Joseph's preaching wandered here there and everywhere. But other times the message was clear and compelling and certainly provided a spiritual alternative for those who were put off by traditional churches with their message of hell and damnation.

There was no question that Increase Joseph wanted people to know about him. Why else would he name the village, the lake, and the stream coming out of the lake after him? Yet, Bakken, thought, he does care about the rest of the community. He preaches for no pay, and makes his meager living farming alongside the rest of the Fellowship's members.

Then there was the matter of the Red Book. Increase Joseph carried it with him always, and claimed loudly and convincingly that it contained the foundation for everything the Fellowship stood for. Yet, no one in the Fellowship, not even Henry Bakken, ever had a glance inside the book. The Red Book had become even more mysterious than Increase Joseph Link.

Finally, there was the matter of the tonic, which was even more secret than the Red Book. Increase Joseph seemed to have an ample supply of this mystical drink, but he only brought it out when someone in the Fellowship took ill, or was injured. Word had gotten around that Increase Joseph carried a bottle of the tonic with him at all times, and when he thought no one was looking, took a long deep drink.

Bakken's curiosity — his newspaper experience provided that — resulted in far more questions than answers about Increase Joseph Link.

Henry and Abigail Bakken had of course attended the dedication ceremonies for the new Standalone Church. Henry was quite taken by Increase Joseph's message, which was clearer than usual that day about what the Red Book said, and what the Standalone Fellowship stood for. Increase Joseph had gone on at length about the threefold relationship of people, God, and the land. The message was simple, clear, and elegant. Every person had the right and the responsibility to develop his or her own personal relationship to God, but should also be mindful that any relationship must include a connection to the land, and to other people.

It was a freeing message, yet one with boundaries as the land and God were givens, never to be doubted in importance, never to be omitted from consideration.

On the following Monday morning, after careful thought, Henry Bakken had summarized what Increase-Joseph said in a front-page story, with the headline: "Standalone Preacher Proclaims New Religion. Advocates Relationship to God, Community And The Land." When the paper came out on Tuesday, its regular day of publication, Bakken sent a copy to the *Milwaukee Sentinel*, a newspaper that had garnered considerable respect around the state since it began publication in Milwaukee in 1837. Much to Bakken's surprise, in a few days he received a letter from the Milwaukee paper's editor, Rufus King, thanking him for the story and asking Bakken to keep the paper informed about Increase Joseph and the Standalones.

"We've been trying to keep a record of various religious groups springing up around the state and this one sounds a little more unusual than most. Can you tell us more about Increase Joseph Link?" King wrote.

Bakken immediately replied with the story of Increase Joseph's message from God after being struck by lightning and about the Fellowship's move from New York.

"I consider Increase Joseph and his family — he has one son — our friends, but he remains a mystery to all of us here in Link Lake. Perhaps a mysterious nature is a characteristic of people destined for fame," Henry Bakken wrote.

In the months and years to follow, Henry Bakken would learn much more about his preacher friend.

Chapter 10
Tent Preaching

September 1852

Increase Joseph penned a letter to his father back in Plum Falls, New York, the first since the Fellowship arrived in Wisconsin. He wanted to report good news but the news was mixed.

The Link Lake farmers started harvesting their wheat crop. They scythed the fields, gathered the grain into sheaves, and hauled them on their wagons pulled by oxen to their log barns where they threshed out the kernels with flails. Because they had arrived to the area too late for ideal spring planting, and because much of their time was devoted to building their barns and cabins, their wheat crop was meager. Some of the Fellowship members worried if they would have enough flour to last them through the coming winter, to say nothing about having something extra to sell. They harvested a few loads of wild hay, scarcely enough to winter their few head of livestock.

Fellowship farmers heard about the harvest in the Willow River community, a few miles south. These Willow River farmers planted winter wheat the previous fall, and were harvesting many more bushels per acre. They sold their extra wheat to the Willow River Mill that was busy grinding flour while the Link Lake Mill stood idle much of the time.

"Next year will be better," Increase Joseph told his followers. "We must have faith."

But Increase Joseph was worried. He knew that he had scarcely enough flour for his family, and he with only a wife and a baby son. Others had many more mouths to feed. The community needed money to buy flour and other food to tide them over the winter. During these trying September days, Increase Joseph walked slowly through the town, his head down and his long arms hanging at his sides. The Red Book was just visible sticking out his back pocket.

On a Sunday afternoon in mid-September, when the Fellowship gathered at the round church, Increase Joseph took his regular place in the fieldstone pit. The fellowship, even during times of despair, knew they could count on their spiritual leader for a message of hope. On this sunny Sunday afternoon, they were not disappointed, although most were surprised at what Increase Joseph said. They opened with their theme, "We Are Alone Together," sung off key as usual, but with considerable gusto. Then Increase Joseph began, "We are gathered here today with thanksgiving for all of God's blessings, in the hope that though today our conditions appear bleak and with little promise, there is always the morrow. There is always the sunrise with its promise."

A great quiet came over the Fellowship as they looked down on their spiritual leader who held the

Red Book in one hand, and what looked like a bottle in the other.

Without warning, Increase Joseph thrust both arms into the air and roared.

"God has visited me in my sleep!"

People could now clearly see that in one hand Increase Joseph held high a bottle of brown liquid—to some it looked like a common liniment bottle.

"God has visited me in my sleep and thrust on me a profound message of inspiration. Do you see what I have in my hands?" he asked loudly.

"I see the Red Book," a little old lady in the front row said. Most agreed that must be the answer Increase Joseph was searching for — the obvious answer as they all, each and every one of them, was guided by this mysterious and sometimes mythical book of beliefs.

"In my other hand? In my other hand?" Increase Joseph asked some what exasperated.

"Liniment?" a lad of twelve or so blurted out.

"You are close to the truth young man. You are close."

Increase Joseph dropped his hands to his sides and bowed his head as everyone watched with a kind of profound reverence. Once again, they would become privy to one of Increase Joseph's visits from God himself. They need only be patient. A minute passed, then several minutes—Increase Joseph was known to drop off to sleep in times like this. Some believed he was searching for a more complete message from on high as if he wasn't quite sure of the original.

Then he shook himself like an old dog that had just crawled out of a lake, raised the hand with the bottle high over his head and said in his deepest, most commanding voice, "In my hand I have a bottle of the most powerful liquid ever known to mankind — Link's Restorative Tonic — some of you know it as I have shared the tonic in moments of sickness and injury. I didn't tell you its name even though you know its power."

Increase Joseph went on at length explaining the heritage of the tonic.

The recipe, passed on for generations in the Link family, originated with an Indian tribe from the northern part of New York State. One winter, when the Indians were near starving, Increase Joseph's distant relative offered the desperate native a sack of corn meal. A few days later the Indian returned the favor with a gourd filled with the tonic. Upon questioning, the Indian proceeded to tell Link, with hand gestures and words, what the ingredients included.

"I have the recipe for this important cure-all in my possession," Increase Joseph said. What he didn't say is that he was the only one who had it and that he kept the recipe well hidden. It was written on a well worn, yellowing piece of paper.

Tonic Recipe
1 quart wild grape juice
1 quart blackberry juice (from the tall kind):
1 handful horseradish root, ground.
1 handful black willow tree, inner bark slivers,
1 handful wormwood leaves, dried.
2 handfuls ginseng roots, crushed.
½ handful catmint, flowering tops
1 wash basin; mullein leaves, dried.
Fresh well water to make five gallons.

Steep mixture over low burning wood fire at least six hours. Stir every half-hour. When steeping done, skim foamy residue from surface with a clean cloth. Bury residue so no animal will taste it.

Cool overnight. Cover kettle so nothing falls into the mixture. The next day pour liquid into gallon jugs. Stop loosely with a fresh corncob. Allow to age for a month unless needed sooner.

"Link's Restorative Tonic brought me back to life after my unfortunate accident several years ago," Increase Joseph continued.

Everyone remembered the time when young Link had been struck by lightning, but they didn't know the tonic's role in restoring his faculties.

"I personally know the power of this tonic," he said. By now people began to wonder what the tonic had to do with Increase Joseph's message from God. As was sometimes the case during the spiritual leader's sermons, the message seemed muddled and off the mark, confused and confounding.

"And now," Increase Joseph roared. "Now my message from God himself from the throne where he reigns with love and compassion." And then silence.

Written over the faces of the Fellowship assembled — what, what message? Minutes passed. People sat on the edges of their seats, watching this great man with the long white hair. This man in black.

"What God told me," Increase Joseph began. "What God told me . . ." He hesitated. "God told me to take my message to all the people, to share what you already so much appreciate. I plan to start next week in Willow River."

Since the article about the Standalone Fellowship and Increase Joseph Link's ministry appeared in the *Milwaukee Sentinel,* several letters a week arrived with invitations to speak to communities around the state.

"Hallelujah!" someone from the back of the church said in a loud voice.

"Thank you brother," Increase Joseph replied

"And there's more," Increase Joseph continued. "God said in a voice so clear that even I could not misunderstand." God said, "Share the tonic! Share the tonic with the needy. Share the tonic with the confused, with the injured both in body and mind. Share the tonic with the infirm. Share the tonic with the heathens and the believers, with fallen women and cheating men. Make no distinctions. Share the tonic. And that's what I intend to do. All profits from the tonic sales will come back to the community. Tonic sales will aid us in buying food and other necessities as we face a long, cold Wisconsin winter."

"Bless you, Increase Joseph," a woman sitting with three squirmy children said. "Bless you," tears were pouring down her face. Others were crying, too. Everyone was worried about the coming winter. Now there was hope.

Increase Joseph, with Bakken's help, had placed an ad in the *Milwaukee Sentinel* for a used, round tent that would seat upwards of 300 people. Henry Bakken wondered why he wanted a tent and now he knew. Increase Joseph planned to go on the road shortly after he received the first letter of invitation several weeks ago.

Increase Joseph asked Henry Bakken to print

up two signs. One, in large red print said, "THE LAND COMES FIRST."

The other sign read in large black type "LINKS RESTORATIVE TONIC." Underneath, in smaller type: "Settles a queasy stomach, calms excitable nerves, quiets an anxious colon, diminishes fever, controls worms, fights rheumatism, improves singing ability, helps to focus attention, makes unhappy people happy, shows the way for those who lack direction, represses headaches, toothaches and ear aches, makes one more attractive to the opposite sex and repels mosquitoes if used externally in sufficient quantity. Fifty cents per bottle."

The ropes were frayed, the once proud tent poles were cracked and bent and some holes in the canvas were as large as a gold coin. But it was a tent and it would seat 300 people, although Increase Joseph had no seats to provide.

"Folks who want your message will be pleased to stand," Henry Bakken said. Henry volunteered to accompany Increase Joseph on his trip to Willow River, to assist in selling the Restorative Tonic.

They started out early on a frosty, clear October morning. The sky was deep blue contrasting with the yellow aspens and the red maples. Long skeins of Canada geese filled the sky from horizon to horizon, a hint of the winter to come. Increase Joseph and Bakken were on their way to Willow River, some fifteen miles to the south. Increase Joseph and his wife busied themselves the previous week readying the remaining supply of the tonic, some 100 bottles. Twenty-four bottles of the magical liquid, the tent, and several feet of challenged ropes and decrepit wooden poles made up the load for the high-wheeled farm wagon pulled by Increase Joseph's skinny team of horses named Dick and Maud. The tent poles were too long for the wagon by three times, so they stuck out the back, occasionally dragging on the ground and sending up little puffs of dust.

Several members of the Fellowship gathered at the round church to see them off and to wish them God's speed. Increase Joseph, and Henry Bakken climbed into the wagon. But rather than sit down, Increase Joseph stood on the seat, the Red Book in his hand.

"A moment of prayer before we embark on this important mission," Increase Joseph said. He loosely tied the driving reins around the wagon's brake handle. The team stood ready, swishing their tails and stamping their hind feet to chase off the flies that tormented them.

"We are off to Willow River, our neighbors to the south," Increase Joseph said, waving the Red Book. He said what everyone already knew.

"We are off to share our message with others who might benefit." A long silence. The horses were becoming impatient.

"We are . . ." but Increase Joseph didn't finish his sentence because a big bumblebee sank its stinger into Maud's rump. She made a giant leap forward, encouraging Dick to do the same and the team, wagon and its contents rumbled down Link Lake's Main Street at a hurried clip. When Maud leaped, Increase Joseph was propelled backwards as if someone hit him with a long stick. He fell in the tangle of folded tent, and became invisible to those who watched the strange departure. Finally, Henry Bakken managed to take up the driving reins and slow the team. By this time they were well on their way to Willow River.

"A wondrous departure! A wondrous departure! God is surely on our side for this great adventure," Increase Joseph said as he found his hat, gathered himself and crawled back on the wagon seat. At this moment, Henry Bakken wasn't too sure whose side God was on.

The duo arrived in Willow River shortly after noon and immediately began erecting their once red tent, which was now a rather sickly faded pink. Neither had put up a tent before and one of this size proved a considerable challenge. Finally, after two hours of sweating and frustration the tent was standing. The south end dipped a little because one tent pole was a bit short, and the ropes, pulled as tight as possible, didn't seem especially sturdy. A few rocks marked the center floor of the tent, the place where Increase Joseph would stand when he gave his message.

With the tent up, Henry Bakken tended the team and readied the back of the wagon for tonic sales. Meanwhile, Increase Joseph strode off toward the Main Street of Willow River, where he announced in a loud voice: "Tent meeting at four this afternoon. A chance to hear God's word. An opportunity to learn a new way."

Dressed completely in black, with long white hair hanging out from the edges of his black hat, he was an imposing figure as he walked with long strides.

He repeated his litany again and again in his booming voice. Storekeepers stood at their doors. Farmers in town for supplies stopped their teams and listened. Children quit playing their street games.

Increase Joseph held high the Red Book, occasionally shaking it and saying, "The message is here, good people. Come to the sacred tent this afternoon and hear more." He pointed toward the empty field on the edge of town where the faded pink tent was scarcely visible.

"Bring your children. Bring your problems. Bring your hopes and desires. Bring your helpmeets and your friends. Bring it all to the sacred tent, and hear the word from the Red Book. Hear the word straight from God."

Increase Joseph returned to the tent, and proceeded to nearly empty a bottle of tonic. He crawled under the wagon and fell into a deep sleep. Shortly after 3 o'clock the first people began wandering into the tent, searching for a place to sit. Several sat on the ground, talking quietly among themselves and waiting patiently to see and hear this strange looking man with his unusual message. Several were more than curious about the Red Book and its contents.

A few minutes before four the sacred tent was nearly filled with curious people. Increase Joseph was nowhere in sight. A few people stopped at the wagon with its large sign proclaiming the virtues of "Link's Restorative Tonic," and five put down their money to buy a bottle, fifty cents each.

Henry Bakken glanced under the wagon and saw Increase Joseph still sleeping. "Increase Joseph," Henry said, gently nudging the spiritual leader. "It's time."

"Time, time for what? Where am I? What is this place?" Increase Joseph said as he sat up, cracking his head on the bottom of the wagon.

"The tent is full. The tent is full of people waiting."

"Who are these people? What do they want?" Increase Joseph crawled out from under the wagon rubbing the lump on his head.

As he stood up, adjusted his hat, and brushed some of the horse hay off his black pants and coat. He found his bottle of tonic, held it up to the light to see that it still had a little in the bottom and drained it.

"I'm ready," he said, brushing his hand across his lips and searching for the Red Book in his back pocket.

He walked into the tent and a great hush came over the crowd. As was his custom, he raised the Red Book high over his head and in his booming voice began: "Brothers and Sisters, welcome to the sacred tent. I am reminded of a time when people gathered to hear the word of God, but were confused about the message. The words were strange and muddled and laced with fearful and foreboding ideas. Yet the people returned each week for they were in search of spiritual guidance and peace of mind.

"Welcome to the word of God that is fresh and unencumbered. Learn how we all may relate to God in our own way, as we relate to each other and to the land."

Everyone was listening attentively, and no one noticed the dark clouds that had been building in the west the entire afternoon.

"I am not here to convert you. I am not asking you to join anything. My message is simple. I am here to assist you. To help show you the way. To help you see that, as a human being, you have the right and responsibility to relate to God as you wish, but at the same time you are always mindful of your neighbor and the land that supports us all."

Those who stood nearest the edges of the tent heard a low rumble of thunder. The afternoon had become unbearably warm in the stillness before the storm.

"Where is your Bible?" A tall, burly, ill-dressed man standing near the front shouted. "Where's your Bible, preacher."

"I have no Bible," Increase Joseph said. "My inspiration comes directly from God Himself."

"What you got in your hand?"

"It's called the Red Book."

"Give me a look, I wanna see what it says."

"This sacred book guides me and instructs me. It is my duty to share its special meaning with each of you. It's my calling." Increase Joseph held the special book tightly, in case someone tried to wrest it from him.

Just then a flash of lighting cut through the black sky and clap of thunder shook the tent. Some of those crowded in the tent began glancing toward the entrance.

"It's all in this special book," Increase Joseph roared in a voice that all could hear above the storm. Raindrops began splattering on the tent as Increase Joseph continued. He seemed oblivious to the pouring rain that began dripping on the crowd through the many holes in the canvas.

Henry Bakken earlier put the tonic under cover in the wagon, and hitched up the team in readiness for their departure after the sermon. He surmised that no one would stand in the rain to purchase tonic. He was sitting under the wagon, out of the rain listening to Increase Joseph's message when it happened. Henry heard a creaking sound, and thought little of it. It was natural for a tent to creak a little. But then he heard a sound like a long barreled rifle report and a moment later saw the tent slowly falling and settling over the crowd. Increase Joseph saw it falling, too, and he promptly turned tail and escaped just before the wet tent blanketed the angry citizens of Willow River who immediately began clawing over each other to find a way out.

Increase Joseph quickly climbed up on the seat where Henry Bakken held the driving reins.

"Drive Henry," Increase Joseph instructed. "Drive as if your life depended on it."

The team and wagon, with bits of horse hay flying, galloped away from the mass of mad humanity that was slowly crawling out from under the collapsed tent. Men and women alike were shaking their fists at the departing wagon that was tossing up clods of mud as the team galloped through the rain.

When the wagon reached the safety of a nearby woods, Bakken yelled "Whoa" to the team. He and Increase Joseph sat in the rain, the water dripping off their hats.

"Better wait here until dark," Bakken said. "Then we can sneak back for our tent."

Long after the storm passed, and darkness had fallen, the old farm wagon with the skinny team quietly returned to the meeting site. Increase Joseph and Henry quickly gathered up the wet tent, broken tent poles, frayed ropes and cracked stakes. They began the journey back to Link Lake.

"A wonderful beginning, Henry. Gloriously wonderful. We have money for our community. Much needed money."

Henry Bakken snapped the driving reins a little, encouraging the team along the muddy road. Henry wanted to tell Increase Joseph that two dollars and fifty cents from their tonic sales wouldn't buy much flour for the Standalone Community, but he didn't say a word. He was thinking about how he would report the results of the trip in his newspaper.

Chapter 11
Not Listening

Henry Bakken didn't know what to make of the tent show fiasco. All his wife, Abigail, could do was laugh when he described the thunder storm and the tent falling on the Willow River faithful and how he and Increase Joseph were hurried out of town.

"Increase Joseph, has a good idea with his tent and tonic selling," Henry said. "But when it comes to practical things, like sturdy ropes and decent tent poles, he is totally inept.

"That's why he has you," Abigail Bakken said, smiling. She was busy working on the advertising spreads for the upcoming issue of the *Link Lake Gazette.*

Henry Bakken left the newspaper office, the little bell on the door tingling as he pulled it open. He hurried along the dirt main street of Link Lake, and up the hill toward the Standalone Church building where he knew he would find Increase Joseph.

Bakken figured he should spend some time with Increase Joseph, trying to console him on their Willow River failure. He also thought he should remind his spiritual leader that perhaps he ought spend less time tending to his spiritual duties and devote more time harvesting his crops. Fall was coming soon to central Wisconsin. Increase Joseph recently scythed his meager wheat crop, but he hadn't yet threshed it. It was piled in one of the two bays of his log barn. In the other bay was the crop of wild hay that he had cut, allowed to dry and hauled into the barn with the help of his pair of old oxen and the noble efforts of his wife, Elwina. They had scarcely enough winter feed for their oxen, team of horses, and the three milk cows that provided them with a minimum supply of milk, butter and cheese. Elwina, quiet and always in the background, not only cared for Little Joe, their son who was two years old, but was saddled with most of the farm work, including caring for the oxen, horses, and milk cows.

Bakken pulled open the church door and in the dim light saw a figure huddled on a church bench in the back.

"Henry, it is you. Sit down. Join me," Increase Joseph said.

"What are you doing?"

"Meditating."

"About what?"

"About how blessed we all are. How fortunate."

"Yes," said Bakken.

"But I have a worry, a deep worry that is tugging at my very being."

"And what would that be?" Bakken asked, surmising that Increase Joseph wanted to lament about the tent show debacle and their meager sale of Restorative tonic.

"It's the people," Increase Joseph said. "It's the

people."

"Which people?"

"Our people, those people, the people here, the people there." Increase Joseph was swinging his arms in a huge arch.

"What'd they do?" Bakken was concerned that Increase Joseph was going off on one of his diversions where he talked on and on, and made no sense at all.

"They are not listening," Increase Joseph said. "Their ears are closed. Their minds are clamped shut as tight as the lid on a pickle barrel."

Bakken didn't know what Increase Joseph was getting at. But something was clearly bothering him. Bakken had come to help his friend thresh his wheat and talk about the future for the tent show ministry.

"What will we do, Henry? Why are our people not hearing?"

"What are they not hearing, Increase Joseph?"

"They are not listening to the land, Henry. The land has a message for all of us, but we must learn to listen, we must hear its message and then heed it. We must capture in our minds what the land is telling us and then act accordingly."

Henry listened attentively, not quite knowing what Increase Joseph was saying.

"It is the core of what we Standalones are about," Increase Joseph continued. "It is the essence of our belief — the relationship of each of us to God, to each other, and to the land."

"I know," Bakken said quietly, rubbing his hand through his red beard and removing his glasses which he proceeded to clean with a red handkerchief.

"On our trip to Willow River I grew increasingly depressed at what I saw. The people around Willow River are clearly not listening to the land, not listening to its message. Did you see those great fields of wheat, stretching out sometimes nearly as far as you could see?"

"I saw the wheat fields," Bakken said.

"Did you see the wind lifting the soil, swirling it up into the air into clouds of dust and sending it on to the east?" Increase Joseph made a swirling motion with his long arm.

Bakken remembered them driving along a stretch of road a few miles out of Willow River where the dust was so thick they could scarcely breathe.

"It is money that drives those people. Money. They are listening to money and ignoring the land. Oh, the futility of their lives. How can they not see what they are doing, Henry? What will it take to unstop their ears, to remove the blinders from their eyes?"

"I don't know, Increase Joseph. I don't know."

"It is our duty. It is our God given mission to take our message out to the countryside, to the villages and farms, to the people nearby and far away." Increase Joseph was now standing, the Red Book in his hand. "We must make sure that our own people do not clear huge fields and plow under all the native grasses, that they do not remove all the trees leaving no shelter for the wild creatures that live there. We must encourage our people to keep listening to the land, as we encourage others to do so."

"Yes," Henry Bakken said in agreement. He wanted to tell his friend that he must also attend to his own family, to his own farming. He wanted to say that they should plan a day soon to visit the tamarack swamps on the north end of Link Lake and cut new tent poles so they could dry over the winter, he wanted to explain that before they set out on another tent show mission the tent canvas needed patching, and the frayed ropes must be replaced. But these were clearly matters that little concerned Increase Joseph.

"Ah, yes, but before we set out next spring we must replenish the supply of Restorative Tonic." Here was one practical matter that Increase Joseph took responsibility for.

Soon after Henry Bakken left, Increase Joseph returned to his cabin, went to the secret hiding place, removed the yellowing, wrinkled sheet of paper his father had given him, and began refreshing his mind on the ingredients and directions for making the tonic. This was after he took a long drink from the bottle of year-old elixir that he carried in the inside pocket of his long black coat.

"Ah, it's this wonderful tonic that will save us all," he said aloud.

Chapter 12
First Winter

Late March 1853

This first winter for the Standalone Fellowship in Wisconsin was long and cold — miserable by anyone's standards. Nearly every week it snowed, starting in November and continuing into the first weeks of March. The snow piled up around the log cabins and around the log barns. It regularly drifted shut the trail that wound along the east side of Link Lake, so that each time someone drove their team to Link Lake they needed to break a new track.

After every storm — some took two or three days to blow out — the cold returned and each time a little more fiercely. To test the cold, Elwina Link would toss a half pail of water outside. One morning she exclaimed, "The water was ice before it hit the ground." No one questioned her statement.

The Fellowship's supplies of flour, beans and cornmeal were nearly exhausted. The last smoked hams were gone and most families had scarcely enough smoked bacon to grease the bottom of a frying pan. During the previous fall and early winter, the hunters in the group—especially the bachelor brothers, Joe and John Judd, and Emil Groskeep, who was far and away the most accurate rifleman in the community, regularly brought in deer, rabbits, squirrels and wild turkeys. But as snow depth increased and the temperature got ever colder, wild game was increasingly more difficult to bag. Walking was difficult, and the game moved some miles away into the deep woods to the north.

The Fellowship began depending on the ice fishermen in the group for food. Andrew Blackwell, Adolph Lang, Frederick Henke and Silas Stewart trudged out onto frigid Link Lake nearly every morning, chopped holes in ice that was three feet thick, and dangled minnows on hooks fastened to thick cords tied to wooden devices they called tip-ups. Blackwell, tall and thin; Lang, with a round head, water blue eyes, Henke with graying whiskers as sharp as sandburs and Stewart, scrawny and frail and perpetually chilled, stuck to their task with the diligence only known by the hungry. They waited by smoky campfires for the red flag on a tip-up to snap up signaling a fish grabbed the bait. These rugged fishermen, sometimes coming off the ice in late afternoon with frost covering their whiskers, hauled northern pike out of the lake, some days twenty or thirty with individual fish weighing up to fifteen pounds. Fellowship wives learned how to bake fish, fry fish, boil fish, make fish soup and fish loaf, and even prepare a fine pike hot dish. Nonetheless, some of the Fellowship men said they'd eaten so much fish that when the ice went out of Link Lake, they would have to resist the urge to plunge in the water and swim off like a northern pike.

The stored hay in the rude log barns diminished to small piles and since bare spots became visible in the fields with the snow melt, the oxen and horses, the chickens and the geese, the skinny milk cows and the razor back hogs were let out to rustle feed on their own.

Even with warmer weather, the nights were still cold, well below freezing and often much colder. The ring of the ax could still be heard in Link Lake and in the farms surrounding. Ever hungry fireplaces demanded wood if cabins were to be at all livable. Wood cutting went on every day until the Fellowship members were becoming exhausted from the constant need to fell oak trees, whack them into reasonable lengths, tote them to their cabins with teams of oxen, and then split the wood into manageable lengths for feeding the never satisfied fireplaces. Would spring ever come? The women in the Fellowship especially wondered. They recalled the winters in upstate New York, and although they remembered lots of snow, they never experienced such cold as they felt in Wisconsin. Many were running out of patience and some began questioning the wisdom of their decision to follow this white haired preacher to the frigid wilds of central Wisconsin.

The women tried to cheer each other. Abigail Bakken tried circle meetings, as she called them. Their purpose was for the Fellowship women to meet at each other's cabins and discuss the teachings of Increase Joseph and the Red Book's contents. At the first meeting, where ten women attended, they discussed Increase Joseph's theme, "The Land Comes First." There were great moments of theological silence as no one knew quite what to say.

"We need a copy of that Red Book," a very pregnant Mabel Blackwell said. "We need something to guide us, something to sink our teeth into."

Mabel, a high strung woman with long hair that hung to her shoulders was frail and intense. Her face was a near constant grimace, no doubt an expression of the back pain she experienced.

"Elwina, you must know what's in that Red Book. What do you have to say?" Esther Stewart asked. Esther was shaped like a corn shock with narrow shoulders and wide hips, and light brown hair that shot out from her head in all directions.

Elwina, not one to say much of anything, sat silent throughout the meeting, fidgeting with a handkerchief she held in her lap. The life of a preacher's wife was always difficult.

"I've . . . I've never been allowed to read it," Elwina said in a quiet voice, her eyes looking toward the floor. "Increase Joseph allows no one to look at it, not even me."

"You don't say," Esther replied.

"I inquired about borrowing the Red Book for our meetings," Abigail Bakken offered, "But Increase Joseph said — and these were his exact words — 'The writings are extremely difficult to comprehend and require higher levels of schooling and a theological perspective.' I said let me have a look and I'll see if I can figure it out. He said that would be impossible."

"He is a strange one," Sophia Trutweiller, the miller's wife, offered. Sophia, plumpish round in every respect, had a smile that spread across her face with the slightest provocation.

"Increase Joseph said that maybe I could take notes at each of his sermons and the group could discuss what I wrote," Abigail said.

"Wouldn't it be better to have the Red Book?" Eleanor Lang asked. Eleanor Lang, a slightly built woman with black eyes and fidgety hands had a voice like a red tail hawk on patrol.

"You'd think so, but you don't argue with Increase Joseph. When he sets his mind on something, he doesn't change," Abigail said.

"I agree with that Abigail," Elwina said quietly.

After three meetings the group disbanded. But they did agree that when Abigail figured she gathered enough notes for a discussion, she'd call the group back together. The winter went on with no future meetings of the Standalone Fellowship Circle.

Some of the women desperately needed to get together, if for no other reason than to share their misery and combat their loneliness. The men ice fished together, cut wood together, and gathered at the Mercantile store in town on occasion. But the only chance for the women to socialize was Sunday at church. Unfortunately, the Standalone Church building was as cold as the inside of an ice house — the Fellowship did not have enough money to buy a stove. The cold winter winds seeped in around the windows and around the door, making church services an ordeal for even the hardiest. Everyone wanted services to end as quickly as possible so they could rush home to their warm cabins.

It was back in mid-March that Elwina got word that the new Blackwell baby was sick, that it had a high fever and a cough. Elwina and Increase Joseph dropped Little Joe off with the Bakkens and rushed over to the Blackwell's cabin that was about a mile down the trail. Mabel Blackwell's face was wrinkled like that of a woman twenty years older. She sat by the fireplace in their cabin, singing quietly to the feverish baby, and scarcely looking up when Andrew Blackwell let the Links in.

Andrew whispered to the Links, "I don't know what will happen to Mabel if we lose another baby. Our first two, a little boy and a little girl are buried back at Plum Falls. When the little girl died two years ago, Mabel nearly went crazy. I don't know what she'll do if we lose this little fellow." There were tears in the man's eyes as he spoke.

"We shall do our best to help," Increase Joseph said.

While Elwina talked to Mabel, Increase Joseph took the Red Book from his pocket and held it to the baby's feverish head. He mumbled some words that no one could quite make out. Then he asked for a spoon into which he poured some tonic. Mrs. Blackwell put the liquid in the baby's mouth, and almost immediately the baby's eyes popped open. It began wiggling its little arms and feet and babbling, as healthy babies do.

"It's a miracle," Mrs. Blackwell proclaimed. "It's a miracle. How can I every thank you."

"It is my mission to serve those in need," Increase Joseph said as he pulled on his long black coat and with Elwina headed back to their cabin.

The next morning there was a loud knock on the cabin door. It was Andrew Blackwell.

"Our baby is dead!" Andrew said. "Died early this morning while Mabel was holding it in her

arms. Didn't cry, didn't shudder. His life just left
him, like a flame disappears when a fire goes out.
Tiny little thing never stood a chance." Andrew's
voice was a mixture of blame and sorrow.

"I'm so sorry," Elwina said.

"What went wrong? What went wrong?" Increase Joseph muttered. He was shaking his head
in disbelief. "The baby took some of the tonic.
He should have recovered. What went wrong?"

"Increase Joseph," Elwina said. No response
from the spiritual leader who stood in the corner,
with his head bowed, muttering "What went wrong?
What went wrong?"

"Increase Joseph," Elwina said again.

"Yes, yes," he replied. "You called my name?"

"We must go to the Blackwells'," She said. "And
offer comfort to Mrs. Blackwell during the time of
her loss."

"Yes, yes, we must," Increase Joseph said. He
was searching his pockets for the Red Book and
his bottle of tonic. "We must go posthaste. Yes,
yes, we must go posthaste to the Blackwells."

Elwina helped Increase Joseph with his coat,
and handed him his black hat. "Yes, yes we must
go," he said.

The day for the funeral dawned sunny and clear,
following several warm days in mid-March that
melted most of the snow. This was the first funeral from the Standalone Church and the first
funeral for Increase Joseph Link. Somehow, in his
conception of what a preacher did, he failed to
realize that funerals and caring for the bereaved
were also his responsibility.

A plain wooden box with the remains of the

baby sat on the little table in the preaching pit. In preparation for the service, Increase Joseph drained an entire bottle of tonic, yet he felt no more ready to face the Fellowship's sadness than had he drunk well water.

The Blackwells were seated in the front row, Mabel Blackwell was sobbing uncontrollably. Andrew sat on one side of her, and Elwina Link, her arm around Mrs. Blackwell, on the other side.

"We remember baby Blackwell on this sunny and warm day. A day when the first flowers are blooming, when the meadow larks are singing, when the bluebirds are searching for places to nest. A day when the Canada geese are winging their way north, calling out their joy for the new season. In our collective sorrow we are blessed that the sun is shining and the snow is melting. That spring is coming once again. Oh, the glories of spring. As we remember the brief life of the one departed, let us look forward to the wonders of new life, as we set aside the miseries of a long and arduous winter. Baby Blackwell will return to the land from whence he came, as each of us will in our turn. Today, we are privileged to look beyond death to the new life of spring."

Increase Joseph, as he continued his message of hope, could not see the dark clouds rolling in from the northwest. As he continued talking in a softer, more consoling voice than his usual style, a cold rain began and almost immediately turned to sleet and then driving snow.

Fellowship members near a window watched as the once nearly bare fields were again buried in white. Increase Joseph went on with his message, holding the Red Book high above his head as he looked upward.

Those members who could see the change in weather wanted to run down and tell him that his message was premature, that winter had returned. But they just sat, bundled up in their winter coats and huddled under thick blankets as Increase Joseph went on . . . and on, proclaiming the virtues of the coming spring and the hope that it brought to all, especially to those experiencing great sorrow.

Finally, the services were over, the last amens were said and everyone walked back into winter.

Increase Joseph was speechless when he saw the fierce snowstorm raging outside. His tonic and prayers failed the Blackwells, and now even his hope for spring had disappeared.

As he walked out the church door, he noticed Elwina, her arm around Mrs. Blackwell, talking to her, consoling her in this time of overwhelming grief.

Increase Joseph walked back to his cabin, dejected. For the first time since the Standalone Fellowship decided to move to the wilds of Wisconsin, he questioned what they had done. He felt like he did the day five years ago after Harvard College dismissed him — a total failure.

Chapter 13
The People From
Pow-Aw-Hay-Kon-Nay

April 1853

Since the baby's death, Increase Joseph began questioning everything that he did, every decision that he made. It didn't help that the Fellowship stored the casket with the dead baby on a shelf in a lean-to back of the church because the ground was frozen too deeply to dig a grave. It would be a week or two before the ground thawed enough for burial, and the first grave in the Standalone cemetery back of the church could be opened.

Each day that Increase Joseph went into the lean-to he saw the little pine coffin. He was reminded of the round-faced, blond haired baby who was such a joy to his parents who previously lost two babies. Increase Joseph couldn't get the death of the Blackwell baby out of his mind. He believed that he, the power of the Red Book, and the tonic should have saved the child. When he saw the Blackwells in church or met them on the street in Link Lake, he had no words for them and could find no way to express his grief and his feeling of worthlessness. They took his standoffish demeanor as not caring, as not being concerned, and they told others about this. But Increase Joseph's feelings were just the opposite; he just couldn't find words or actions to express what he felt so deeply.

For hours on end, Increase Joseph sat in front of the fireplace in his cabin, ignoring Elwina and Little Joe and staring into the Red Book as he slowly turned the pages. He was looking for an answer, searching for a sign.

To make matters worse, one day, after the recent snow melted and green grass began appearing on the south sides of his cabins, Increase Joseph awakened with a severe headache and runny nose. He had not been ill during the entire first winter in Wisconsin, but this sunny morning in April he was sick. Immediately he took a long drink of the tonic and returned to his bed to allow the wonderful elixir to do its work. At noon he felt no better and by nightfall he felt absolutely awful. Once again, the tonic failed. Was God punishing him for his errors and shortcomings, for his blunders, for his inability to be what he knew he was capable of being? "Give me direction. Open a door for me," he quietly prayed.

A soft knock came to their cabin door. Elwina got up from her rocking chair near the fireplace, where she had been knitting and opened the door. She gasped, stepped back, and put her hands in front of her face.

"We . . . mean . . . no . . . harm," the tall, thin dark skinned man with black hair and deep set brown eyes said in halting words. He was clad in buckskins from his feet to his head.

"I Kee-chee-new. We Menominee, people of Pow-Aw-Hay-Kon-Nay," The tall, fine featured man, with high cheekbones and prominent nose said, carefully speaking each word. He was accompanied by a younger, shorter man who said nothing, but smiled and nodded when the tall man spoke. The shorter man also wore buckskins and was carrying something folded over his arm. Three-year old Little Joe, who was playing on the floor, jumped up and ran behind his mother, glancing out from behind her long full skirt.

"Is . . . this . . . house . . . of . . . Link?" the man asked. He was glancing around the cabin.

"Yes," Elwina said quietly. Fear was etched on her face. She knew she was facing an Indian and didn't know what to expect.

"Is headman Link here?" the tall Indian asked. "We look for headman Link."

Increase Joseph overhead the conversation from his bed behind the curtain in the back of the cabin. He got up, overcame a bout of dizziness, and slowly walked to where Elwina stood at the door.

"I am Increase Joseph Link." The spiritual leader extended his hand to the tall Indian. His voice was hoarse.

"I Kee-chee-new," the tall man said. "You are headman Link?"

Increase Joseph smiled. His head throbbed and he knew he had a fever.

"I am a preacher," Increase Joseph said. "A spiritual leader."

"Spirit leader?" Kee-chee-new asked. He looked puzzled.

"Well, yes, perhaps." Increase Joseph answered. He had not heard preaching described in quite this way.

"We camp by the lake, our men and women and children. We camp there many times before on journey from trapping lands to trading post on river Fox." Kee-chee-new waved his arms toward the west, the direction of the marshy lands, and then toward the east, where the Fox River and Berlin were located. The Standalone Fellowship briefly visited the trading post at Berlin and had taken the Ferry across the Fox River, on their way to Ames County.

"Come into our home," Increase Joseph said. "Enter and rest." He pointed the two men toward chairs, but they remained standing.

"How can we be of assistance?" Increase Joseph felt another wave of dizziness and he steadied himself by the side of the table. The tall Indian was watching him closely.

"We need salt, Kee-chee-new trade for salt." He turned to the young man standing at his right and took a tanned fur from him.

"We trade skin of the wolf for salt. You trade with us headman Link?"

"I would be privileged to help someone in need. Elwina, get these men some salt." Elwina walked to the corner of the cabin that served as a pantry and came back with a small sack of salt and a plate of cookies. Little Joe, his eyes wide with excitement, stayed next to her.

Kee-chee-new handed the bag of salt to the younger man.

"Have a cookie," Elwina said, handing the plate to the tall Indian.

"Cookie?" Kee-chee-new repeated; he looked puzzled.

"Good," Increase Joseph said. He smacked his lips, in a chewing motion. The demonstration succeeded in making his headache worse.

The shorter Indian took one of the white sugar cookies and bit off half of it. Immediately he smiled. Kee-chee-new likewise took a cookie from the plate and began eating.

"Good," he said. "Good." Both Indians stuffed the remainder of the cookies in their mouths.

"Good," Kee-chee-new said again.

Increase Joseph unfolded the wolf skin revealing a soft, carefully tanned pelt that was silver gray in color.

"We are privileged to receive this fine wolf skin. We shall cherish it always," Increase Joseph said. He sat down in a chair, with the wolf skin on his lap and wiped his hand over his hot forehead.

"You not well, headman Link?"

"A fever has overtaken me," Increase Joseph replied. "It came upon me last night and it remains."

"I have cure," Kee-chee-new said. He reached within his leather outer garment and produced a small leather pouch that was filled with liquid.

"Take drink, it good for you. Cure fever."

Increase Joseph wanted to tell this tall Menominee that he had been taking his own special tonic, a tonic that originated with an Indian tribe in northern New York State. But he didn't have the strength to go into a long explanation.

Increase Joseph took a long drink of the medicine and handed the pouch back to its owner. He wiped his hand across his mouth. The drink was more tart than his tonic, but otherwise possessed a similar taste.

"You feel better soon," Kee-chee-new said. "Fever go away."

"Thank you," Increase Joseph said.

As quickly and quietly as they came the two Indians left. Elwina watched them walk toward the lake. In the distance she could see several thin threads of smoke, which must be their campfires.

The following morning Increase Joseph awakened without a headache and no fever. He was curious what gave Kee-chee-new's tonic such potency. He knew he must find out.

Later in the day Increase Joseph walked the trail to Link Lake and stopped at the office of the *Link Lake Gazette*. He was certain that his old friend had further information about the Indians who stopped by his cabin. He told Henry Bakken about his experience, and about the potency of their tonic.

"Did you get a name?" Bakken asked. He rubbed his hand through his red beard and adjusted his glasses.

"Man in charge called himself Kee-chee-new. Said his people were from Pow-Aw-Hay-Kon-Nay."

"Lake Poygan, they were people from Lake Poygan. Menomonees. They call the lake Pow-Aw-Hay-Kon-Nay. Read about this somewhere," Bakken said. "I know about Kee-chee-new, too; he's one of their chiefs."

"Friendly fellow, looking for salt." Increase Joseph said.

"The Menomonees sold the last of their land back in '48, to the U.S. Government. We're standing on what was once theirs."

"Their land?" Increase Joseph said.

"It was; some of them don't realize that they're not supposed to traipse around here like they used to," Bakken said. He was busy setting type for the weekly edition of the newspaper.

Increase Joseph shared the story of his illness and fever, and how the tall Indian's tonic cured him while his own didn't.

"Must be powerful stuff," Bakken said, not looking up from his work.

Increase Joseph made up his mind to find out what the additional ingredients were. Soon he would be taking his tent ministry on the road, as warmer weather arrived. A more powerful tonic would surely sell well. The Fellowship helping fund, made up of tonic profits, was always short of money it seemed.

"Let me know if Kee-chee-new and his people come back this way," Increase Joseph said.

"I surely will," Henry Bakken said. The smile on his face revealed his knowledge of what was going on in the spiritual leader's head.

By the third week in April, spring arrived with a rush. The Standalone Fellowship farmers were busy plowing their fields with their teams of oxen, sowing spring wheat and oats, and readying their gardens for planting. One warm day, with temperatures in the seventies and a brisk wind from the southwest, the ice on Link Lake began piling up on shore and melting, once more revealing the pristine blue waters.

On a warm afternoon, Increase Joseph and his reluctant team of oxen were plowing the small acreage that he cleared back of his cabin. Even though he had grown up on a farm, he never quite captured the skills necessary for plowing and for doing most farm work. Yet, just because he was the group's preacher did not excuse him from farm work. He received no salary from the Fellowship, and no money from tonic sales, beyond necessary expenses, so the farm provided his family with their meager living.

At times he knew he was the brunt of neighborhood jokes about his poor farming approaches. He even learned that the better farmers in the Fellowship often looked to how he farmed as a guide for what they should not do. Word got back to him that this was happening, but he didn't let it bother him much. He knew his mission was preaching.

He was sweating profusely as he tried to guide the stubborn oxen across the small field. He wished his farm language was as persuasive as his preaching language. Some of his neighbors, even though they were God-loving men, had words that the oxen seemed to better understand. He knew he should probably remind these men that including the name of the Lord in yelled commands was not appropriate. But their oxen kept the plows turning over the fresh soil, and his oxen mostly stood eating grass and looking at him with mournful eyes.

He noted a figure coming up the trail to the cabin and recognized Henry Bakken.

"Good to see you, Henry," Increase Joseph said, wiping a handkerchief across his brow.

"How's the plowing going, Increase Joseph?" Henry asked, smiling.

"Wondrously well. Such contented oxen I have. So relaxed. Makes my work more pleasant."

"Those beasts are surely relaxed," Henry said, laughing.

Henry Bakken noted that Increase Joseph plowed but two furrows in the three acre field. At the rate he was going, he would still be plowing when his neighbors were harvesting their crops.

"I have news for you," Bakken said. "Kee-chee-new and his people are back."

"Kee-chee-new? Who is he?"

"The Indian you told me about."

"Yes, yes, Kee-chee-new. The man with the powerful tonic that cured me."

"He and his people are camping north of here, on the lake. Don't know how long they'll be there. Saw them trailing through town."

"Thank you, thank you, Henry." Bakken left and Increase Joseph immediately unhitched his oxen from the plow and put them in the little corral back of the barn.

"Have we got anything I can give to the Indians? A gift of appreciation," Increase Joseph asked as he stopped by the cabin. He told Elwina what he learned from Henry Bakken as he glanced at the huge wolf skin, a gift from Kee-chee-new, that he had hung above their fireplace.

"Just baked an apple pie with the dried apples we had left," Elwina said. "And we still have lots of salt."

"I'll take the pie and some salt," Increase Joseph said. "Apple pie will make an especially fine gift, a token of my thanks and my friendship."

Increase Joseph set off down the trail toward the north. He could see the campfires by the lake and soon spotted the shelters. As he got closer, he saw that some of the men were wading in the lake with long handled spears, gathering fish that the women were cleaning and hanging on wooden racks to dry.

Near naked children were playing in the dirt, dogs were barking, women were scurrying around. The camp was a busy place on this warm afternoon in April.

When they saw Increase Joseph coming, everyone stopped what they doing. Except the dogs that ran up to Increase Joseph, barking furiously at his arrival.

Chief Kee-chee-new saw Increase Joseph, too, and slowly walked over to him, a big smile spreading across his face when he recognized the visitor.

"Spirit man Link," Kee-chee-new said. "Your illness has passed."

"Indeed it has. I am fit and well, thanks to your glorious tonic. And I have gifts for you, tokens of my appreciation. More salt and an apple pie."

"Apple pie?" Kee-chee-new said quizzically.

"It is good. You will like it."

Kee-chee-new stuck a long finger in the pie and put some of it into his mouth. "Good. Good," he said.

Increase Joseph noticed that Kee-chee-new was stirring something that was cooking over a smoky fire.

"Making more medicine," Kee-chee-new said. "Almost finished."

The two men, Kee-chee-new carrying the apple pie as carefully as he would something that would break, and Increase Joseph still toting the small bag of salt, walked toward the steaming iron kettle, no doubt recently acquired at the trading post in Berlin.

"Need crane berries, and sugar from the maple tree. Otherwise mixture complete," Kee-chee-new said.

Increase Joseph noticed that Kee-chee-new carried a small bag of dried red berries; he looked at them carefully. They were cranberries. Some of the Fellowship picked wild cranberries the previous fall, from the marshes not many miles south of Link Lake. Several members of the Fellowship tapped maple trees on their farms and enjoyed the maple syrup. And they had cooked maple syrup in upstate New York.

Perhaps these were the "secret" ingredients in Kee-chee-new's tonic. He couldn't wait to get home, take the recipe from its secret place and brew up a new batch of his own tonic, but this time adding maple sugar and cranberries.

He said goodbye and headed back up the trail toward his cabin. He turned once to wave and saw Kee-chee-new stuffing handfuls of apple pie in his mouth. The tall Indian was smiling broadly.

Chapter 14
Spiritual Challenge

Summer 1858

Five years passed quickly. With the new recipe, enhanced by the addition of maple sugar and dried cranberries, tonic sales soared. Profits from the tonic allowed Increase Joseph to buy a new and larger sacred tent, and wooden bleacher seats so his followers could sit comfortably while they listened to his message.

After expenses, all the money from tonic sales went into the Tonic Helping Fund. Almost every year, someone needed assistance from the Fund. One year Joe and John Judd received several dollars. Joe broke his leg when an oak tree that he was sawing fell on him. Word was that it was no accident as the boys didn't get along that well. But nonetheless, Joe couldn't do much work that summer. With tonic money, they hired a man from Willow River to help with heavy field work. Another year, a small grant went to Henry Bakken when one of his newspaper presses broke down and he couldn't scrape together enough money to have it repaired.

Just last year, Silas Stewart put in for tonic

money when his wife nearly neutered him with a butcher knife while he was sleeping. The Fellowship elders discussed the request for two long nights before they voted six to four in favor. Some said that Silas, who always had an eye for younger women, got what he deserved. But the majority agreed that Silas needed money to tide him over until he healed, even though the morality of his actions wasn't exactly in accord with the values of the Standalone Fellowship.

With the success of his tent ministry and tonic sales, Increase Joseph's confidence returned. Seldom did he think of that first, awful winter in Wisconsin when the Blackwell baby died and the Fellowship had scarcely enough food to see them through until spring.

Each year the Fellowship farmers cleared a few more acres and planted a little more wheat and corn, always making sure to keep their fields small. For several years they were able to sell extra wheat at the Link Lake Mill that was working every daylight hour grinding the grain into flour. They hauled wagon loads of flour to Berlin where it was loaded on the recently completed railroad that connected to Milwaukee via Ripon. Most of the farmers bought new wood stoves for cooking and heating their cabins. The Blackwells and the Bakkens even replaced their log cabins with new frame houses from lumber sawed at the Link Lake Sawmill. A new black stove with shiny chrome trim stood in the back of the Standalone Church that had new doors and new calking to keep out the cold.

Increase Joseph's message of land-God-people was well received as he took his tent and tonic to such places as Grand Rapids on the Wisconsin River, and north to Plover, and south to the Portage, where Indians and French traders had once hauled their canoes from the Fox River to the Wisconsin and then paddled on to Prairie du Chien, a major trading post on the Mississippi.

At every gathering, people lined up at the tonic wagon, as Henry Bakken sold bottle after bottle of the elixir. Unfortunately, some people came, bought a couple bottles of tonic — still 50 cents a bottle — and then left before hearing Increase Joseph's message.

Henry Bakken informed Increase Joseph that this occasionally happened.

"Their leaving makes room for those who want to hear my message," Increase Joseph said. "I know the day will come when they, too, will enter the sacred tent. They must first be ready. Not everyone is ready to hear my message. There is a right time. No one knows when it is. But when they feel the need, when the time is right, they will come. And we will be ready. We will welcome them with open arms."

Henry Bakken smiled. He was always impressed with Increase Joseph's optimism, even when it was misplaced.

John Pardee, who ran the flour mill in Pardeeville some forty miles or so south of Link Lake, inquired if the great spiritual leader might bring his tent, tonic, and message to his community. He knew many people would turn out.

"I'm surprised," Henry Bakken said when he heard about the invitation. "That part of the state has several Bible churches and your message might be a bit threatening to them."

"John Pardee said nothing of this," replied Increase Joseph. "We have not been to this place, and I think we should go."

They loaded their new round tent, which was large enough to shelter nearly 500 people, the new seats, and several cases of tonic. They pointed their two wagons toward Pardeeville, passing through Willow River on the way and remembering the inconvenience of their old tent falling on the faithful at their first tent meeting. They traveled past mile upon mile of wheat fields, stretching sometimes as far as they could see. With spring rains, the wheat was green and growing, and had just headed out.

They stopped after an hour or so of travel, at a little fast-moving stream where they watered and rested their horses. Increase Joseph and Henry Bakken sat under a huge white oak tree that stood alongside the well-traveled road.

"Fields are too big. Too much greed here. Farmers trying to do too much," Increase Joseph said. "Their inappropriate tillage approaches will catch up with them."

"Looks like everything is going well," Henry Bakken said as he waved his arms in the direction of a substantial wheat field near the road.

"Ah, but it will change. Mark my words, Henry; it will not always be so. The land, like a she bear protecting her cubs, will rise up and strike back. And the attack will come as a surprise, when least expected. The land will rebel at the time when people think they have subdued it and have it doing their will. Never underestimate the power of the land, Henry. Never."

"We'd better be on our way," Bakken replied.

The men climbed back on their wagons and continued their journey toward Pardeeville and the several nights of tent sermons planned for that community.

Arriving in Pardeeville they stopped at the mill where they met John Pardee.

"Delighted to see you," Mr. Pardee said. "Found a place for your tent just outta town. Good place. Oak trees for shade. People can rest their teams in the shade." Pardee's clothes were covered with white flour dust.

"I'm sure you have selected well," Increase Joseph said.

The two men from Link Lake spent the next two hours, with some help from three Pardeeville young men, erecting the tent, setting up the bleachers, and making the tonic wagon ready..

When the work was done, Bakken and Increase Joseph sat under the big oak trees resting, eating some sandwiches they brought with them, and enjoying the pleasant day.

"I have a grand feeling about this week," Increase Joseph said. "A grand feeling. We are in a new place, with new people. People who have not heard my message. People who have not had an opportunity to experience the wonderful attributes of our tonic."

Henry Bakken put a couple more sticks on the little campfire they built to warm their tea. He stared down into the flames, but said nothing. So far, Increase Joseph had been fortunate, Henry thought. Most people applauded what he said, even though he knew many had no idea what he was talking about. They were mesmerized by his speaking style, and that was good enough for them.

A reason for attending.

With each sermon, Increase Joseph brought a sharper edge to his message, which potentially could make enemies of those who disagreed with him. He did not preach from the Bible, and that alone alienated those who thought that a religion was false unless it depended on the Bible for its inspiration and message. The Red Book, which Increase Joseph depended on for his information and insight, remained a mystery. No one, except Increase Joseph himself, knew what words it contained, what messages it held beyond those already shared by the great man in black.

Increase Joseph's message sounded innocent enough, until one listened carefully about what caring for the land meant. It was more than saying "I love the land," or "We are from the land and to the land we return." These were just words, and almost anyone would agree with them. But, Henry thought, when Increase Joseph talked about farmers' greed, as he did while taking a break on their way to Pardeeville — few people would agree with him. Henry wondered if his preacher friend was at all aware of the direction his ministry was taking him, and the consequences that might occur when people began understanding his message and began talking back, or worse, began taking actions against him.

"Henry, you are so quiet. What thoughts are passing through your mind?" Increase Joseph asked.

"Nothing really," Henry lied. "I'm just enjoying the beautiful day and our company together."

"It is a fine day," Increase Joseph agreed.

John Pardee posted signs all around Pardeeville, at the livery, in the country store, at the hardware, in the several saloons, and of course at his mill.

"Increase Joseph Link. Free lecture. For the entire family. Learn about a new way for living your life. Limited seating. Seven p.m. at the round red tent south of Town." And in smaller type, "Link's Restorative Tonic available at .50 per bottle."

By six p.m., people were already lined up to buy tonic, and the back seats in the tent were filling rapidly. Increase Joseph stayed out of sight under his wagon. He tacked up a curtain to enclose the space. He sat, hunched over in the limited area, paging through the Red Book and planning for the evening performance. Every few minutes he took a drag from a bottle of tonic, which he each time replaced in the inside pocket of his black frock. As he often did, after several minutes of contemplation he fell asleep, oblivious of the huge crowd of people that filled the red tent to capacity with many standing in the back, waiting for the appearance of the famous spiritual leader.

"Increase Joseph, Increase Joseph," Henry said as he knocked gently on the side of the wagon.

"Yes?" Increase Joseph said. His voice was barely audible.

"It's time," Henry said quietly.

"I'm sleeping," Increase Joseph answered. "I am not to be disturbed."

"There are hundreds waiting for you in the red tent."

"Hundreds?"

"The tent is full, Increase Joseph. They are waiting for your message."

"I am not ready," Increase Joseph said. "I am in the center of my preparations."

"You must come. People are beginning to clap their hands. We are already nearly ten minutes late."

Increase Joseph dug in his pocket for his bottle of tonic, took a long drink, crawled from under the wagon and pulled on his black hat. He brushed the timothy hay from his black pants and walked confidently into the tent. Now the clapping changed to loud welcoming applause.

The great man in black took his place at the center of the tent and raised both arms over his head in response. In one hand he held the Red Book. The applause was near deafening. People obviously heard about his ministry and his message and flocked to see and hear this great man in person.

Finally, he motioned for them to be seated, and a long silence ensured before he began speaking. Increase Joseph noticed several men standing in the back of the tent were not clapping and had sour expressions on their faces. He thought little of it as he began his message.

"We are each of us like the giant oaks that we see just outside this tent," he began.

"The oak lives in harmony with its neighbors, the aspen, the maple, and the pines, as we each must learn to live with those who are different from us." Heads were nodding in agreement.

"We must learn how to live in harmony with the Norwegians and Welsh, the Swedes and the Danes, the Irish and the English, the Poles and the Germans, and with Indians, too, like my friend, Chief Kee-chee-new of the Menominees. All are our neighbors.

"We must learn to live with those whose work is different from ours, whose celebrations differ from ours. We must learn to live with those who worship in ways foreign to us. There is one God, and He is concerned about all of us, no matter how we chose to honor Him. He wants us to prosper, but He wants us first to respect the land and then respect each other."

A loud voice came from a man standing in the back. He was part of that small cluster that was not clapping and cheering. The man was built like a long-necked buck sheep with flared nostrils.

"What is that book you are holding?" the man shouted. His voice was as cold as yesterday's campfire. Several heads turned to see who was speaking.

Increase Joseph was taken by surprise because he wasn't accustomed to being interrupted during his message.

"Why. . . why it's the Red Book," Increase Joseph said. "And why do you ask?"

"Is it not the Holy Bible?"

"No, it is the Red Book," Increase Joseph responded.

"Do you not draw your words from the Bible?" the man continued. He was so intense that the muscles on his neck vibrated.

"My guidance comes from God and from this book." He held the Red Book high over his head, moving it back and forth so all could see.

"You are a fraud, Increase Joseph Link. A humbug. You are speaking false truths. You are taking the name of our Lord in vain, blaspheming Him, denigrating Him, using Him to sell your wicked tonic," the man bellowed.

"Oh, kind sir," Increase Joseph began.

"I am not your kind, sir," the man interrupted.

"I welcome your comments," Increase Joseph said calmly. "As I welcome perspectives from everyone."

"You have no right to speak, you messenger of the devil," the angry man said in voice that nearly shook the tent poles. People sat stunned, except for a few who were enjoying the exchange.

Increase Joseph stood quiet for a moment, and then in a strong, confident voice continued, "I come from God with a message for all, including you sir." The man seemed out of breath so Increase Joseph continued.

"We are all on this earth together, and we must learn to respect and love each other, no matter what our beliefs, no matter what our background, no matter what the color of our skin, or the books that we read, or the holy men that guide us. There is no right way. No single way. There are many ways."

A huge round of applause erupted spontaneously from the audience as many of them jumped to their feet, clapping loudly.

"Blasphemy! Blasphemy!" The unhappy man in the back said. "You will die in the flames of hell you Antichrist." He shook both fisted hands at Increase Joseph, who stood facing him and smiling.

The heckler and his band of followers disappeared into the night. Increase Joseph continued for nearly an hour, holding the vast audience spellbound.

Later, Increase Joseph asked John Pardee about

the man who interrupted him.

"Oh, that's Pastor Magnus Overight. He preaches at the Holy Bible Church and is looking for new members. An angry man. I stay away from him."

Increase Joseph and Henry Bakken, extremely pleased with their evening work, sat by their smoky campfire, eating their sparse supper and looking at the expanse of stars that stretched from horizon to horizon.

"A great time to be alive, Henry," Increase Joseph said.

"You handled the heckler well," Henry said.

"God knows what I am doing and appreciates it," Increase Joseph responded.

"Sometimes I'm not so sure," Henry said, as he drained his cup of tea and prepared to sleep in one of the wagons. Increase Joseph spread out his bedroll in the other wagon.

In the middle of the night, Henry Bakken was awakened by the smell of smoke. The red tent was on fire.

"Increase Joseph, the tent is burning," Henry yelled.

Both men stood in the night air as huge flames rose from their big canvas tent. Its waxed waterproof canvas burned like pine kindling in a fireplace. In a few minutes, what had been a new tent with new wooden bleachers was a pile of ashes.

"Apparently Magnus Overight's anger was even greater than we thought," Henry Bakken said.

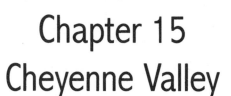

Chapter 15
Cheyenne Valley

November, 1859

Nine year old Little Joe began accompanying his father on his forays around Wisconsin, selling the tonic off the back of their wagon. Little Joe was developing a gift for selling that was only exceeded by his famous father. But like his father, when he wasn't in front of a group, he was extremely shy and reserved.

Many people were enthralled with the quality of Little Joe's voice, "And he's only a kid," they said. Some came to hear Little Joe's sales pitch outside the tent over the spiritual message his father delivered inside. There was something about the thin, fine-boned little boy who stood on the back of the wagon shouting out, "Buy your Link's Restorative Tonic here. Only fifty cents a bottle, two for a dollar, Remember, Link's Restorative Tonic is good for your stomach and for your nerves. It will fight the rheumatism and improve your singing ability. If you a have a tendency toward unhappiness, it will make you happy. If you got a toothache, a headache or an earache — this here tonic will take care of it. Do away with those hurts as fast as you can say 'I'm cured.' And if mosquitoes have been bothering you, rub on a bunch of Link's Restorative Tonic and they will disappear. Won't bother you no more. Some mosquitoes tip right up on their backs when they come in contact with the tonic."

The youngster memorized the message so well he never missed a word when he repeated it again and again. He wore a white shirt, with red bands around his arms, and a huge black cowboy hat. And all the while he talked he waved a bottle of the tonic over his head, in the same fashion that his famous father waved the Red Book when he preached. Some claimed that it was the attraction of the youngster that brought as many people to the sacred tent as did the now famous spiritual leader from Link Lake.

On one of those rare days when Increase Joseph and the tent ministry were not making a public appearance somewhere, a letter arrived in the offices of the *Link Lake Gazette* for Increase Joseph. People regularly sent mail to the spiritual leader in care of the newspaper. Some were addressed to "Preacher Link," some to "Tent Preacher, Link Lake, Wisconsin," others to "Spiritual Leader, Standalone Fellowship, Ames County, Wisconsin." One even came, "The Man in Black, Link Lake, Wisconsin."

Henry gave the letter to Henrietta to run up the hill and give it to Increase Joseph. As usual, Increase Joseph was sitting on a back bench in the church, thumbing through the pages of the Red Book, something he did often.

"Ah, another correspondence," he said when he saw the letter in Henrietta's hands. "Another person requiring my services." He unfolded a long-bladed jackknife that he carried in his pocket, and slit the envelope open. He read it carefully, not saying anything.

"Tell your Pa, thank you," he said as he dismissed Henrietta, who was the same age as Little Joe and cute as a "bug's ear" as someone in the fellowship said.

The letter was from Walden Stewart, Cheyenne Valley, Bad Ax County Wisconsin, a two day's travel from Link Lake.

"Dear Preacher Link, I have heard about your message and applaud your good work," the letter began.

Increase Joseph read it carefully, for the message seemed different from many he recently received.

"I know that Bad Ax County is a long way from Ames County. But would you consider paying us a visit? You need not bring your tent; or your assistants we want only to spend time with you. We also have a highly secret matter to discuss. Let me hear soon that you will come.

"A fellow traveler on this earth,

"Walden Stewart.

"Cheyenne Valley."

Increase Joseph quickly penned a reply and walked the letter down to the Link Lake post office. He immediately made plans to set out for Bad Ax County, located on the western edge of Wisconsin.

Once in hilly Bad Ax County, he made but one inquiry at a country store and was directed to Walden Stewart's place. The farm was in a valley of fertile farmland, far richer soil than the sandy hills owned by the Standalone Fellowship in central Wisconsin. The valley was surrounded by rather steep hills, the tops of which were covered with what appeared to be excellent timber—oaks, ash, hickory, walnut.

Increase Joseph drove his horse and buggy up a long twisting drive to a neat but modest farmstead consisting of a log home, a log barn and several other log outbuildings. He tied his horse to the hitch rail and strode up to the porch, the Red Book in his hand. He knocked on the door and it was opened by a gray haired black man with a deeply wrinkled face.

"Welcome," the black man said. "You must be Preacher Increase Joseph Link. We've been expecting you."

"Ah . . .hello," Increase Joseph stammered. "You . . . you're a black man. Is Walden Stewart here?"

"I am Walden Stewart." he said. "Have always been a black man." A big smile split his face revealing two rows of irregular white teeth. "Glad you came."

"How . . . How'd you come to Wisconsin?" Increase Joseph said, the surprise not yet erased from his face.

"Born in North Carolina. Move to Illinois. Live there twenty years. Raise my kids in Illinois. Had a hankering to move further north so we moved here a few years ago. There's a bunch of us black folk living here now, in this valley."

"Well, Mr. Stewart, I am pleased to shake your hand. Pleased indeed. Never shook the hand of a black man before. Never have."

"Call me Walden," Stewart said.

"I will do that, Walden. I will be happy to do that."

That evening, several other black families from the community gathered at the Stewart cabin to meet with Increase Joseph and ask him questions about his ministry.

"Our farms do well. We raise wheat and oats. Have some cattle, too," Walden Stewart began. "But some of our fields are steep. The rains are washing away our soil."

"Yes," Increase Joseph said, listening intently.

"How do we stop the gulleys? How do we stop the washing?" a young black man asked. "We just be'in hornswoggled by the rainy weather"

"You ask important questions," Increase Joseph said. "The land is our foundation. It is the basis for our existence. To worship the land is to worship God."

"We know, Preacher Link, but what do we do to save our soil and still raise crops?"

A deep silence settled over the modest cabin. The only sound was oak wood crackling in the fireplace. Increase Joseph sat with his hands folded over the Red Book, his eyes closed. After a few minutes, one of men whispered to a woman sitting next to him, "I think the preacher be asleep."

Just then Increase Joseph's eyes snapped open.

"I have the answer," Increase Joseph said. "Plow around the hills rather than up and down them."

"Plow 'round the hills?" the young black man asked, looking surprised at what he was hearing. "Plow 'round the hills?" someone else asked. He had a big grin on his face.

"Yes, plow according to God's plan, plow around the hills."

"But everybody plows up and down the hills."

"Follow God's plan to respect the land. Plow around the hills and your soil will remain in place. It will not wash away."

"Any other suggestions?" Walden Stewart asked.

"No," said Increase Joseph. "Except now we must pray. Dear Lord," he began. "We are gathered here this evening in your presence to learn how to form a brotherhood with the land. We must learn to plow around the hills rather than up and down them, Amen."

Several of the people were shaking their heads in confusion. They had expected a more fancy and much longer answer to their questions.

"Could we discuss one other matter, Preacher Link?" Walden Stewart said quietly.

"Yes, of course."

"We have brothers and sisters who are slaves in the South. They are but chattel of their masters. They work long hours, are often brutally beaten, and their children are sold and their families destroyed."

"I have heard," Increase Joseph said.

"We need your help," Stewart said. "We need you . . ." Increase Joseph waved his hand to interrupt.

"I stand ready. The color of a person's skin is not important. The content of his heart is what matters. What do you want me to do?"

"Have you heard of the Underground Railroad?"

"No . . . don't believe so. Where is its headquarters? What do its trains carry?"

Walden Stewart laughed. "It's not a real railroad. It's a way to help our escaped brothers and sisters reach Canada where they are free. But the slave catchers follow them. These miserable bounty hunters chase them wherever they go. We need you and your fellowship to provide a way station. A place for our brothers and sisters to rest and be nourished. We need your help to carry them on to the next station. It's dangerous. Slave catchers lurk in the shadows. Always ready to make their move."

"I'll do it," Increase Joseph said without hesitation.

"Bless you, Preacher Link, Bless you." Walden Stewart said. "Someone will visit you soon and tell you more. And do not share any of this except with those who need to know and you trust."

Everyone shook Increase Joseph's hand as they filed out of the cabin and on to their own farmsteads. It was a clear, crisp evening with stars shining brightly in a cloudless sky. A sliver of oak smoke trickled from the Stewart cabin's chimney. A hoot owl called from deep in the woods along the nearby hillside.

Chapter 16
Underground Railroad

Early November 1859

Henry Bakken was the only member of the Standalone Fellowship who subscribed to the *Milwaukee Sentinel*. Even though he received the paper a few days late by mail, it kept him current on happenings in the state as well as nationally. Many stories in the *Sentinel* he rewrote and included in the pages of the *Link Lake Gazette*.

He read in the *Sentinel* of turmoil developing between the northern and southern states. It was clear to Bakken that slave ownership in the South was creating deep rifts in the federal government and throughout the country. Earlier he read about the 1820 Missouri Compromise. This resulted when northern and southern congressmen debated whether slavery should be allowed in those vast territories west of the Mississippi River. He remembered that Missouri had been allowed slaves but the other lands of the Louisiana Purchase were not given that right.

He read of the Fugitive Slave Act of 1850 that allowed bounty hunters to go after escaped slaves and return them to their Southern owners. He learned about the great anti-slavery, anti-Southern feelings this law created in the North.

Henry Bakken thought these events would never involve him, or the Standalone fellowship that was trying to keep body and soul together in the wilds of Wisconsin. As a result, he included only the briefest mention of North-South strife in the *Lake Link Gazette*. That is until he read what happened at Harper's Ferry.

The November 9th issue of the *Link Lake Gazette*, on the second page, carried this headline: "John Brown Tries to Seize Federal Arsenal." The story continued. "On the night of October 16, 1859, John Brown and several of his followers attempted to seize the Federal Arsenal at Harper's Ferry, Virginia. The marauders' intention was to steal the weapons stored there, place them in the hands of southern slaves, and start a slave insurrection in the South. Brown succeeded in holding the arsenal until the morning of the eighteenth. On that date, a Marine detachment, under the command of Robert E. Lee of the U.S. Army succeeded in overpowering Brown and his followers. Brown awaits trial for treason."

A short time after the John Brown story appeared in the *Link Lake Gazette*, Increase Joseph returned from his trip to Cheyenne Valley in western Wisconsin. He told only his wife, Elwina, of the details of his visit. When Henry Bakken inquired, Increase Joseph told him that the trip was about plowing around hills rather than up and down them. With no further information, Henry was puzzled, but this was not the first time.

A couple weeks later a well-dressed man in a

horse drawn buggy arrived at the offices of the *Link Lake Gazette* on Main Street.

"I'm looking for Preacher Increase Joseph Link," the rather serious looking man with a white beard said. He limped and walked with a crooked wooden cane.

"Try at the round log church at the top of the hill," Henry Bakken said. "When he's not out preaching, you can find him there, puttering around." Henry did not think it unusual for a man from out-of-town to visit Increase Joseph.

"Thank you sir," the well-dressed man said. He climbed back on his buggy seat, gently snapped the reins and headed up the hill toward the church.

"Anyone about?" the man inquired when he arrived at the church, opened the door and stepped inside.

"Down here, in the preaching pit," Increase Joseph answered. He climbed up the fieldstone steps and walked toward the man with the cane.

"And who might be calling on Increase Joseph Link this fine day?"

"Name is Josiah Longstreet," the man said. "Can I sit? My bad leg's giving me fits today."

"By all means good sir, have a seat. Are you a man in need? Do you require direction in your life? Can I help with your bad leg?"

"As a matter of fact I am looking for assistance. You were referred to me by Walden Stewart."

"Stewart, Stewart, don't think I know a Walden Stewart."

"He's the black man you visited a few weeks ago."

"Oh, Yes, Walden Stewart. Nice man. Interested in the land. Going to plow around the hills rather than up and down them."

"He told you about the Underground Railroad," I believe, Longstreet said in a near whisper.

"Ah, yes.   A way to help out our poor black brothers and sisters from the South."

"Precisely," Longstreet said, wondering if this rather absent minded preacher was someone who could really help his cause.

"I stand ready to assist everyone," Increase Joseph said.   "I provide words of inspiration and hope, words of caring and consideration. And we make available, for a small sum, our famous Restorative Tonic that has improved the health of thousands and assisted in providing a sense of clear direction for many more. Perhaps I could interest you in a bottle of tonic for your bum leg."

Josiah Longstreet ignored the sales pitch and began talking about the African slaves who lived under unbearable conditions in the South. He told Increase Joseph about the hundreds of people like himself, sometimes under great danger, who were assisting escaped slaves on their way north to Canada.

"We need the Standalone Fellowship to help us keep the Underground Railroad running," Longstreet said. With his long thin fingers he was rubbing his obviously painful knee. "We need you and a few of your members to provide brief shelter and food as our Negro brothers and sisters search for sanctuary and ultimate freedom. And we need someone to drive them to the next station."

Longstreet went on to explain some of the history of the Underground Railroad and how it worked. "We use some of the language of the rail-

road," Longstreet said, "Those who transport the
fugitive slaves are conductors, the slaves are called
packages, and the safe houses are known as sta-
tions. The Underground Railroad, of course, is
neither a railroad nor underground. But we get
the work done, quietly, and efficiently."

Increase Joseph was quiet for a moment, staring out the window of the church toward Link Lake.

"How many escaped slaves?"

"We never know. Sometimes weeks go by and
there is no one. Then five or ten will come at a
time, and the following day a similar number."

"And the risks?" Increase Joseph asked.

"It's dangerous business," Longstreet said.
"When slaves are on the move, bounty hunters
follow trying to capture them so they can haul the
poor souls back South. If you're caught harbor-
ing a slave, they'd soon shoot you as not."

"I've heard enough," Increase Joseph said holding up his hand. "This is something we must do. I
will inform the elders of the Fellowship on Sunday, and the following week we'll be ready to receive our Negro brothers and sisters."

"You are doing the right thing, Preacher Link.
Thank you. Josiah Longstreet stood with some
difficulty and extended his hand.

"Wait a moment, I have something for you," Increase Joseph said. He soon returned carrying a
bottle of brown liquid.

"Here's a bottle of Link's Restorative Tonic, my
gift to you. It will do wonders for your bad knee."

"I'll try it," Longstreet said, smiling. He hobbled
toward the door, climbed into his buggy and drove
out of town.

The following Sunday afternoon, immediately

after services, Increase Joseph asked the ten elders of the church, including Henry Bakken to stay behind for a brief meeting. These meetings were held on occasion. It usually meant someone in the Fellowship had stepped out of bounds and corrective action was needed — perhaps a personal visit from one of the elders was required. Or perhaps someone needed financial assistance from the Tonic Helping Fund.

But this was not the usual gathering of elders to discuss someone's personal indiscretion or emergency need.

Increase Joseph took his place in the preaching pit and lifted the Red Book high over his head, holding it with both hands. This was something that he seldom did.

"The railroad's a' comin'," he said quietly. "The railroad's a' comin' to Link Lake."

Not even Henry Bakken, the newspaper man, had heard about a railroad coming to town, so this was clearly news. But what did it have to do with the Fellowship?

"The railroad's a' comin' from deep in the South, it's rumbling through the valleys and climbing over the hills, it's chugging through the small towns and past the little farms. It's a railroad without a train. But it's filled with passengers." Increase Joseph stopped for emphasis.

"The railroad's a' comin' and it's carrying slave people who are searching for freedom, African slaves who toiled under the hot Southern sun picking cotton and feeling the sting of the whip when they faltered.

"The railroad's a' comin' and we've been selected as a station, a stopping off place, where the passengers can eat and rest before we transport them on to the next station on their way North.

"The railroad's a' comin' and we must not tell a living soul, for if we do we will be in grave danger, and so will our guests, because there are dangerous men who try to track them down and take them back South.

"The railroad's a' comin'. Listen and we can hear it. We can hear the wail of the infants, and the sobs of the mothers whose children have been sold. We can see the ribbons of scars crisscrossing the backs of the field hands.

"The railroad's a' comin' and we are a part of it."

Increase Joseph sat down, removed his black hat and ran his fingers through his long white hair.

"How soon before they'll be here?" Henry Bakken asked.

"Soon. A week, maybe two," Increase Joseph answered. "We must be ready. Beyond the usual, I have already decided that each adult coming this way will be given a free bottle of tonic. It will help them keep their eye on the North Star, and ward off any illness that may attack them."

The elders of the Standalone Fellowship filed quietly out of the church. To a person they agreed with Increase Joseph's request. More often than not, the elders couldn't agree on anything — it was the way of the Fellowship. But not this time.

Chapter 17
Isaac and Caroline

Sunday, November 27, 1859

A slow, drippy cold rain began falling shortly after sunrise and continued throughout the day. It could have easily been snow. The leaves of the aspens and the maples in and around Link Lake that had been so colorful but a few weeks earlier had fallen. The trees, like naked sentinels, stood watch over the lake and the little village of Link Lake tucked up against the south shore.

The Standalone Fellowship farmers finished cutting their long rows of corn nearly a month earlier, yet some of the corn shocks still marched across the fields like Indian teepees. Each day the farmers hauled a few of the ear rich corn stalks into their barns where they husked out the yellow cobs on the threshing floor.

The wheat crop was especially good this year — most of the Fellowship farmers harvested several acres. The bins in their granaries were full to overflowing. The Link Lake Mill, water powered, ran from early morning until late afternoon grinding wheat into flour. For the last several years,

there was more than enough flour for the Fellowship families, enough so the mill could sell what
was becoming a famous brand—Standalone Premium Stone Ground Flour — on the open market
with a percentage of the profits going to the
Standalone Fellowship. The emblem on the flour
sack was that of a tall thin man, clothed in black
with his arms lifted over his head. In one of his
hands he held a small red book. People came to
associate Standalone Premium Stone Ground Flour
with Increase Joseph, his preaching, and his famous tonic. Rainwater gently dripped from Increase Joseph's cabin roof as nightfall settled over
the land. He sat in a straight backed chair on one
side of the fireplace that crackled and snapped
and sent cozy warmth into the modest room that
served as kitchen, dining room, and living room
for him, his wife and their son, Increase Joseph II.

Elwina Link sat on the other side of the fireplace,
in a rocking chair. She was knitting a new pair of
mittens for Little Joe. A ball of gray wool yarn lay
at her feet. Little Joe was reading in his *McGuffey
Reader*, homework from the Link Lake School
where he was in fourth grade. A big brown dog
lay at his feet dozing, soaking up the warmth of
the fire. He had no name and was simply called
"Dog," or when he was out around town, The
Preacher's Dog.

Increase Joseph was thumbing through the Red
Book, stopping occasionally to look into the fire.
A gentle knock on the cabin door. Dog lifted his
head. Little Joe turned toward the door; Elwina
Link stopped knitting. No reaction from Increase
Joseph.

"Increase," Elwina whispered.

No response.

"Increase," she said more loudly.

"What, what?" Increase said, his face turning toward her.

"Someone's at the door."

"At the door."

"Yes, at the door.

"Why is there someone at the door?"

"I don't know."

Increase Joseph slid the Red Book into his pocket and stood up. Dog walked with him to the door.

Increase Joseph, in his usual flamboyant fashion, threw the door open wide and the man with the cane, who was about to knock a second time almost fell into the room. He was wet from the top of his slouch hat to the tips of his leather boots.

"May I come in?" he said, a surprised look on his face.

"You, you look familiar. I've seen you before. At one of our Great Gatherings maybe?"

"I'm Josiah Longstreet," the man whispered. "I stopped by a few weeks ago inquiring about the railroad."

"No railroad around here. You must have the wrong place."

Rain continued to drip from the cabin roof, squarely on top the man's head.

"The Underground Railroad."

"Underground Railroad? Ah, yes. Now I remember. Yes. Yes. Why are you standing there with water dripping down your neck? Come in the house."

"I've got some packages in my wagon, can I bring them in?

"Sure, yes, sure. Retrieve your packages. Ah, the packages."

Shortly, Longstreet was back at the door with two blanket clad figures beside him. He followed them into the Link cabin.

"This is Isaac," Longstreet said. "And this is his wife, Caroline. They have come all the way from Tennessee."

Caroline, a small black woman with short hair and fine features was shivering uncontrollably. Elwina went to her, helped her remove the wet blanket and put a chair near the fireplace for her to sit and warm up. She found a dry towel and blanket.

"I'll heat some soup left over from supper," Elwina said.

"Thank you ma'am. You are kind people," Caroline said as she rubbed her hands together in front of the flames.

Isaac, a tall, thin, black man was in his late twenties. He removed the dripping blanket from his shoulders and walked to the fireplace and stood behind his wife, warming himself from the flames that leaped from the chunk of oak wood that Little Joe took from the wood box and placed on the fire.

"Best I can figure, the slave catchers are only a few hours behind us," Longstreet said.

"Slave catchers?" Increase Joseph said.

"Mean bastards, too. They already shot at us once, but we managed to give 'em the slip. Gotta get these folks to Green Bay, get 'em on the steam ship 'Michigan.' Captain Stewart'll let 'em off in Canada. Once they warm up a little and get some grub in 'em, I suggest you get on your way."

"Where do I take them?" Increase Joseph inquired.

"There's a farm on the west end of Lake Poygan, at the end of the road. Look for two candles in an upstairs window. Get them there before daylight, drop them off, and turn right around and come back."

"I am more than happy to help those in dire need," Increase Joseph said as he shook Josiah Longstreet's hand. Without even stopping to warm up, Josiah Longstreet, hobbled out to his buggy and soon disappeared into the cold rainy night.

"Joe, come help me harness the horses," Increase Joseph said as the two of them headed off to the barn. The smell of vegetable soup began filling the small cabin as thunder rolled in the distance and rain continued splattering on the cabin windows. The young couple relaxed somewhat. Each ate a steaming bowl of soup along with several slices of homemade bread. They had little to say. It was obvious they were frightened as they stole quick glances at each other, but said little.

In a short time Isaac and Caroline, warm and with full stomachs, found themselves in the back of Increase Joseph's big wagon that he used to haul his tent and other equipment. He covered them with the tent canvas, and on top of that he placed several bundles of corn stalks. If someone stopped to inquire, he would say he was hauling corn to a friend's farm.

But no one stopped them as they sloshed along the muddy roads on the way to Lake Poygan, the next station on the Underground Railroad. The rain stopped sometime after midnight, and a stiff wind began blowing from the north, portending

colder days to come. Just as the first streaks of
light began appearing in the east, Increase Joseph
spotted Lake Poygan in the distance and soon
found the little farmstead with the two candles
burning in the cabin's upstairs window.

Increase Joseph helped the young black couple
from under the corn stalks and tent canvas and
hurried them to the door where an older couple,
who were up and waiting, showed them into the
house.

"I have something for you," Increase Joseph
said. He handed a bottle of tonic to each of them.

"Drink this for good health, and Godspeed to
both of you,"

Increase Joseph turned, hurried back to his
wagon, and drove well past noon before he arrived
home. He was not prepared for what greeted him.

Chapter 18
Slave Catchers

November 28, 1859

Increase Joseph's horses walked with their heads down, slowly moving along the wet rutted road toward Link Lake. Increase Joseph, dozing as the team plodded along, was bone tired but pleased that he had become a part of the Underground Railroad and its dangerous but important task.

When the horses began speeding up, he knew they were getting close to home. Horses have an extra sense about their home barn, and no matter how tired they were, always hurried to get there. A stiff wind blew out of the north, sending slate gray clouds skittering across the sky, the remnants of the previous day's storm. The November sun hung low in the sky, trying to warm the countryside but without much success. As Increase Joseph neared Link Lake, he saw waves sending up small towers of spray as they pounded the many rocks that were scattered there. The wind sighed as it sifted through the naked branches of the aspens and maples scattered along the lake shore.

In the distance, at the flour mill located where

the river tumbled out of the lake, he saw men at work, unloading wagons heaped high with sacks of wheat. As he guided his team down Main Street of the village, he noted a few buggies parked in front of the Mercantile store, and another team and wagon tied to the hitch rail in front of the lumberyard. A typical Monday in the village Increase Joseph thought as he continued on his way toward his farm and the Standalone Church that stood on the knoll just above his cabin.

Then he spotted something unusual. Two saddle horses were tied to the hitching rail in front of the *Link Lake Gazette*, horses he didn't remember seeing in and around Link Lake before. Just as everyone in a small town knows everyone else's kids, dogs, and wagons, one also knows their horses. One of the horses was gray, the other black. Both stood with their heads down, a sign that they had been ridden hard for many hours. A rifle scabbard hung on the side of each saddle, something unusual in this area because no one carried rifles on their horses. A blanket roll was tied to the back of each saddle — clearly the riders of these horses were travelers.

He rode on past the newspaper office, curious, but not too curious because Henry Bakken, by virtue of his position as newspaper editor, often had out-of-town visitors.

Increase Joseph could see his cabin ahead, a trickle of wood smoke coming from the chimney. The clouds had all but blown away and the sky was the color of the lake, as was often the case in late fall. The finger of gray smoke from his cabin chimney contrasted with the blue. Increase Joseph breathed deeply and sat up straight. Even though he was tired, he felt good, knowing that he had done something important.

As he passed a cluster of big white pine trees, he was startled when a youngster dashed out and ran to his wagon. It was Henry Bakken's daughter, Henrietta.

"Stop, stop," Henrietta said excitedly.

"Whoa," Increase Joseph said, pulling on the horses reins.

"They're lookin' for you," Henrietta said. Her face was flushed.

"Who's looking for me, someone in distress, someone who needs help?"

"Slave catchers are lookin' for the town preacher. They're at Pa's newspaper right now, waitin' for you to come back. Pa sent me up here to warn you."

"Why would I need warning? I am a man of the cloth."

"They think you hauled a slave couple out of here last night."

"They do, huh?"

"Yeah, and they got guns. They're wearing guns strapped to their belts and they're mean lookin'. Pa thinks you should hide somewhere until they leave, maybe drive out to Andrew Blackwell's farm and hide in his barn until the slave catchers leave town."

"I will not hide from these men. I will confront them and share with them the word of God, and show them the error of their ways."

"Pa thinks they'll shoot you dead, like a stray dog."

"I will face these men without fear young lady. You go tell your pa what I said."

Increase Joseph said "Giddy up" to the team and they continued on up the hill. Where before Increase Joseph was chilled, now beads of perspiration appeared on his forehead. He reached into his coat pocket and took a long drink from a bottle of tonic. He wiped his hand across his mouth, then took another drink before putting back the cork and sliding the near empty bottle into his pocket. He noticed that his hands were shaking.

Elwina Link stood at the open door as Increase Joseph said, "Whoa" and climbed down from the wagon, stretching his long arms skyward.

"It's a glorious day, Elwina. A day that the Lord has made." He tried not to show that fear gripped him to the very core of his being.

"Henrietta Bakken said some mean looking men inquired about you."

"I heard," Increase Joseph said. "When they come, show them to the church."

Increase Joseph went to the pantry off the kitchen, found two more bottles of tonic, and headed for the church just up the hill.

"You be careful," Elwina said.

"I am a man of God," Increase Joseph said. "I am protected from harm as long as I believe, and my beliefs have never been stronger."

"You be careful anyway," Elwina said.

Increase Joseph was sitting on a bench near the preaching pit when the church door flung open and the two men burst in. One, tall and heavy, had a black patch over one eye and a long mean looking scar that started at the patch and continued down to his chin. He wore a gun that hung low from his belt. The second man, shorter and older, had a gray beard and wore a crumpled, dusty hat. He, too, had a pistol shoved into his belt.

"You the preacher man," the fellow with the beard growled.

"I am Increase Joseph Link, man of God," Increase Joseph responded.

"We heard runaway slaves have come to Link Lake," the man with the patch said.

"Of what assistance can I be to you men? Are you troubled, are you seeking direction in your lives?"

"Just shut up with that crap, and tell us where you took those runaways," the bearded man said.

"You sound troubled my good man, have you sought out God. Have you lost your connection to the land?"

"You tell us what we want or you'll be meeting your maker sooner than you intended," the man with the patch said, fingering the handle of his gun.

Little Joe crept into the church from a back door, and stood near his pa.

"Get that kid outta here, we mean no harm to the youngster," black patch said.

Increase Joseph bent down and whispered something into Little Joe's ear and the youngster promptly left. Then Increase Joseph picked up the Red Book and lifted it high over his head.

"There are bad feelings in this room, evil feelings," Increase Joseph said, taking on his preacher pose. "Here are men who are misdirected, who have lost their way. Here are men who would take away the freedom that all of us are entitled to, no matter what our color. Here are men who need my help, who could benefit from my teaching."

The two men looked perplexed. Here was someone not afraid of them and with the guts to stand up and lecture them.

Increase Joseph went on, his eyes closed, the Red Book held high over his head. "Care for these men, God. Try to understand them. Look for a way into their hearts for there is goodness in each of us, yea, there is goodness in these men, too. Help them in their moment of need to see how they must reconnect to the land."

"To hell with it," black patch finally said. "This is a crazy man." The duo stomped out the church and climbed on their horses that were tied to the hitching rail.

They hadn't ridden but a few feet when both horses began bucking violently, nearly throwing the riders to the ground. Gray beard's crumpled hat flew off his head and landed on a pile of fresh steamy horse manure.

The horses then began galloping down the road, the men yelling "Whoa! Whoa!" but with no response. Soon they were out of sight.

Increase Joseph and his son watched them leave.

"Horses sure liked the tonic, Pa."

"Appears they did," Increase Joseph said.

Chapter 19
Sandstorm

April 1860

The sun came up granite red in a hazy sky
that Monday spring morning. Almost no rain
had fallen since the last remnants of winter
snow had disappeared in early March. A hot wind
from the west blew steadily, night and day, since
the beginning of April.

The huge wheat fields to the south and west of
Link Lake were on the move. The wind was lifting
the sandy soil in dirty swirls and sending it high
into the sky in brown, menacing clouds that
tumbled over on themselves as they scudded east.

Women could no longer wash their clothes and
hang them on clotheslines to dry as they were
soon dirtier than before they were washed. Dust
as fine as flour seeped through the cracks around
the closed cabin windows and accumulated in little
brown piles on the window sills.

The Standalone farmers, most of them anyway,
had listened to their spiritual leader and plowed
smaller fields broken up by patches of woods and
natural growing shrubs such as hazelnut, wild
grape and blackberries that grew among the split

rail fences that enclosed the fields. The dry wind spared these acres because to do damage the wind needed distance, required a vast area to gain momentum. This was the case for the big wheat fields to the west of Link Lake that were being pummeled by the harsh spring winds.

The Standalone farmers' wheat, planted the previous fall, survived the cold winter well, and although the crop could surely use some rain it was still green and growing.

Increase Joseph, and Little Joe, now ten years old, packed their two bright red high-wheeled wagons for a week-long tour of communities west of Link Lake, in the heart of wheat growing country. A couple years ago, using tonic sale profits, the Links had added a second wagon and bought another team of horses. One wagon carried the round, red sacred tent, tamarack tent poles, tent stakes, ropes and seats. The second wagon carried an ample supply of "Link's Restorative Tonic." This wagon also had sufficient room so the Links could sleep in it. The tonic wagon looked much like the covered wagons that hauled settlers from the East. It was covered with a white canvas that was stretched over wooden hoops that were some four feet high in the center. Printed on the canvas on each side of the wagon in large letters were the words, "Preacher Increase Joseph Link. The Land Comes First." On the wagon's back gate, in blue letters was written: "Link's Restorative Tonic. You Have A Problem? Here's The Answer? Fifty Cents a Bottle, Two Bottles for a Dollar."

Several farmers from Buffalo Creek, Wisconsin, several miles west of Link Lake, invited Increase Joseph to come, expressing their horror of what was happening to their wheat crop and to their lives. They stated great confidence in what Increase Joseph would be able to do for them in their hour of despair.

The two wagons headed west into the dusty haze of the early morning. Increase Joseph, driving the tent wagon, was first. Little Joe followed with the tonic wagon. As the wagons trailed on, the sky became ever thicker with dust and the sun slowly disappeared like a fading lamp in a dark night.

The horses plodded along, their heads down. Increase Joseph and Little Joe tied bandanas over their faces so that only their eyes peered out. As they drove along the road that skirted a vast wheat field, they couldn't see the heads of their horses at times. The blowing sand, worse by many times than blowing snow, stung their faces and tore at the horses' hides

"Whoa," yelled Increase Joseph to his team. Little Joe stopped his horses with their noses nearly touching the tent poles that stuck out the back of the front wagon. Increase Joseph felt along the side of his wagon until he reached Little Joe's team.

"Can't see where I'm going," the preacher yelled to his son. The howl of the wind prevented easy conversation. "Can't pick out the wagon tracks, they're all buried in sand."

"Been following your wagon close, Pa," Little Joe said. "Sometimes your wagon just disappears into the cloud of dust and I wonder if I've lost you."

"I'll lead the team," Increase Joseph said. "I'll walk in front and see if I can find the way."

"I'll keep following your wagon," Little Joe said,

pulling his kerchief higher up on his face. Any fear he expressed was hidden by the kerchief.

"We'll die out here if we don't keep on going," said the famous preacher. "I've been praying to God, but I've got a feeling he wants us to keep struggling on, and that's what we're going to do."

Slowly the two wagons and their drivers rumbled across the vast flat area of wheat fields. It had become a moving hell of dust and grime.

One time Increase Joseph led the team off the road. He didn't notice until he discovered the ground was much softer underfoot and the wagon wheels were sinking even deeper. Back on the road they continued until finally discovering they were in the town of Buffalo Creek, the destination for their first stop. The dust was so thick in the air, it was like night. Main Street of the town was deserted, but here and there a dim lamp light shone through a dusty window. They stopped their teams in front of the general store and went inside.

A plumpish woman wearing her gray hair in a bun was busy dusting a wooden counter.

"Howdy," she said. "Nobody in two days has stopped here. How'd you make it through the storm? Fellow yesterday said the roads were about drifted shut with blowing sand. By the way I'm Evangeline Everts."

"Name is Increase Joseph Link," the spiritual leader said as he pounded dust off the sleeve of his black coat. "This here is my son, Little Joe."

"You're the preacher man we been expectin'" the woman said excitedly as she came from back of the dusty counter and extended her hand.

"I am Preacher Increase Joseph Link," the man in black said. "I am here to aid those in need, cure the infirm, show direction to those who have lost their way, and to remind everyone that they are of the land."

"We sure don't need remindin' about that last part. Everybody in town has some of the land in their eyes, in their ears, in their homes, in just about everything. We need your help to save us from this calamity," Evangeline said, her tone once more serious.

"I am here to help. To do what I can. Where can we erect our sacred tent, where it will be out of the wind, and protected from the blowing sand?"

"Just out of town there's a grove of trees. Bunch of us decided that you could put your tent up there and you'd be out of the wind," Evangeline said. "Just keep on headin' out of town on Main Street. It's right there. You can't miss it. Old Henry Jackson lives in a shack in the shade of them trees. His boys'll help you put up your tent. Bless you, preacher," Evangeline said. "Bless you." She tried to put her arms around the spiritual leader, but he quickly turned and headed for the door. Over his shoulder he said, "Four o'clock. Tell everyone to appear at the sacred tent at four this afternoon for my message."

The two wagons rolled out of town and then the dust miraculously cleared and they could see. There was blowing dust behind them and blowing dust a distance ahead of them. The oak woodlot split the dust storm and provided a small area of quiet. They picked out the little cabin in the clearing and before they could say "whoa" to their teams, four sturdy boys came piling through the door and ran out to meet them.

"Howdy there, preacher man," the bigger boy

said. He was tall, well muscled and his red hair
shot out in every direction.

Before an hour passed the sacred red tent was
up, the seats erected and the tonic wagon backed
into place.

"Thank you young men for your gracious welcome and your ample assistance. You are entitled
to front row seats this afternoon during my presentation. And one more favor. Run through the
town and tell everyone we are here and to come
for my spiritual message at four o' clock."

Increase Joseph walked back of the tent wagon,
took a bottle of tonic from his pocket, drained it
and crawled into the back of the tonic wagon. Soon
he was sound asleep; exhausted from his challenging trip from Link Lake. He was awakened by the
sound of voices. It was Little Joe selling Restorative Tonic off the back of the wagon, and doing a
brisk business as people were standing in line
waiting to plunk down their coins.

All the dust must have created a great thirst,
Increase Joseph thought as he felt for his Red Book.
He climbed down from the wagon and strode into
the sacred tent, which was nearly filled with people
from town and beyond, many of whom must have
braved the rigors of the sandstorm to arrive.
Within minutes the tent was filled, and Increase
Joseph motioned to Little Joe to cease tonic sales.

The great spiritual leader, dressed in black from
head to foot, walked to the front of the tent and
lifted both arms high over his head. A hush immediately came over the large audience.

"I have answered your appeal for help," Increase Joseph began, "to bring words from the Red
Book to help you see through your dilemma and

be on your way to living rich and fulfilled lives."

"Amen," a burly farmer from the back row said. "Amen."

"As it is my custom with my flock back in Link Lake, I often ask for exclamations of need from my followers, expressions of pain and discomfort, disclosures of wants and desires. Who will be first to speak? Who will stand up and be recognized in the midst of this great dust storm that has enveloped us?"

"I'll talk," a tall thin man sitting near the back said. He was rubbing his eyes. "I grow wheat. Have for years. My wheat's ruined by this infernal wind that blows day after day. Stop the wind, preacher. Make it rain. Use your power."

"And who is next," Increase Joseph said, scarcely recognizing the first man's comments.

Evangeline Everts from the General Store stood up. "Our regular preacher said that God is punishing us for our sins. People believe him. Granary Saloon has almost no customers. Card playing is nonexistent. Some have even quit smoking and one man confessed to not sleeping with his wife until this calamity passed." There was a slight titter in the audience from the last comment.

"Anyone else have something to say," Increase Joseph asked looking out over the audience.

Silence. Increase Joseph lifted the Red Book high over his head.

"God is not punishing you for your sins," he said in a voice that seemed to make the tent canvas vibrate.

A great burden seemed to lift from the shoulders of those present. A relaxed look appeared on the faces of many. They expected to hear another tirade about how God was unhappy with their personal transgressions.

"God is not the reason for your punishment. You are."

A stunned silence. People were straining to make sure they were hearing correctly.

"Your punishment comes from your own doing. You have turned under vast acres of land, destroying the trees and the shrubs. You have given the wind an opportunity to gain power as it whips across your huge fields and tears out your wheat plants and lifts your soil into huge black clouds that roll to the east."

More stunned silence. People couldn't believe what they were hearing. They wanted prayers of deliverance, prayers for the wind to stop, prayers for the rains to start.

"This is your own doing. You have no respect for the land and now you are paying the price."

He lifted the Red Book high in air. "These are the words of truth. "Look in the mirror. Blame what you see. You have brought this calamity on yourselves."

"Fake," the word came from the wheat farmer who stood up earlier. "Fake," someone else joined in. Soon there was a roar that rose from throughout the tent as people got up to leave. "Fake, Fake."

Increase Joseph stood with his hands at his side, not responding. Angry people hurried out of the tent. The words, "Fake, Fake, you're no preacher," hung in the air.

The tall, thin wheat farmer who was still rubbing his eyes walked up to Increase Joseph and stood in front of him.

"You get out of town, you fake preacher in black." He raised a hand to hit Increase Joseph, but didn't. "You skedaddle on out of here as fast as you can. If this tent is here come sunup, I'll burn it down myself." The thin man stomped out the tent.

Increase Joseph and Little Joe spend half the night taking down their tent and packing up the seats and other equipment. They decided to return home after this chilly reception in wheat country. They were not looking forward to the long trip back to Link Lake, through the sandstorm and howling wind. As they finished hitching the teams to the wagons, they noticed that the wind had quit, and in the distance they heard the rumble of thunder. As they drove their teams down Main Street the first drops of rain began falling on the parched earth. Increase Joseph pulled his hat down further on his head and turned up the collar on his black coat. He was smiling.

Chapter 20
A Nation At War With Itself

Spring 1861

The headline splashed across the top of the first page of the *Link Lake Gazette* read: "Our Nation Is at War With Itself." The story continued,

"On April 13 Southern guns opened fire on poorly defended Fort Sumter at the entrance to Charleston, South Carolina's harbor. The bombardment continued for most of a day before the little garrison surrendered. President Abraham Lincoln immediately issued a call for the states to provide the federal government with 75,000 men. They are to serve three months."

Increase Joseph Link, now 38, was himself a candidate for service. So were many of the men in the Standalone Fellowship. He called a meeting of the Fellowship for late afternoon.

When everyone gathered, Increase Joseph, in his usual black garb, strode to his place in the fieldstone pit. As was his custom he carried the Red Book that he held high over his head.

"Most of you have heard that we are a country at war. Our nation will pit brothers against brothers, fathers against sons. Blood will run red on our hillsides and in our valleys. Wives and mothers will weep over their losses and a great wound will be opened in this country that will take generations to heal. No country can fight with itself without suffering losses that will extend beyond the imagination."

He stopped to allow the enormity of the situation to settle over the group. Everyone was watching him, waiting for his next words. He continued speaking more softly than his usual preaching voice. "As a Fellowship of believers, we must decide our course of action, because mark my words, the day will come that we will be asked to serve. We will be asked to put down our plows, take up our rifles and march south with orders to kill."

A great pall of black silence settled over the small group of farmers and tradesmen that gathered in the round church, like dense smoke from a forest fire engulfs everything in its path.

Increase Joseph, his voice scarcely audible in the back rows, went on. "The Red Book says we are all brothers under the skin, white and black, red and yellow, Southerners and Northerners. Everyone is entitled to believe in his own way, to act out his beliefs as long as they do not interfere with others."

Not a murmur from those gathered. A few heads were shaking in agreement.

"We have come here from New York State as a Fellowship so we could each believe as we wished to believe, so we could act each act on our beliefs as we saw fit. Our motto of standing alone as we stand together has served us well. To be true to our beliefs each of us has a right to stand up and say whether we will take up our rifles and fight in this war or refuse and suffer what will surely be serious consequences."

The silence continued. The only sound was that of a lone robin outside the open window, singing a song of happiness and expectation of warmer weather to come.

"Those who do not wish to take up arms and fight in this civil war, will stand up and be counted. Women, too, stand if you are against your men taking up arms."

In an instant, everyone in the room was standing, men and women, boys and girls. Everyone.

"Once more we are standing alone together," Increase Joseph said. "May God bless us for our brave action. Please be seated."

A few people were headed for the door, on their way home to do the evening chores.

"One more thing," Increase Joseph said. The people near the door sat down.

"Once our neighbors hear of our action some will spit at us, some will try to harm us; most will curse us and call us unpatriotic. Stand your ground. Look them in the eye and explain why you have done what you've done, why you believe as you do. Say to them that people work out their differences by talking and negotiating, not by killing and maiming.   But do not criticize what they believe and what they do, for they have that right, as you have the right to your beliefs. These could be the most difficult times we have faced. We will face them with our heads held high and with our hands at our sides."

There was some obvious fidgeting in the seats. What Increase Joseph was saying now hadn't yet

occurred to many of the people who a few minutes earlier stood on their feet and declared their
opposition to war and its consequences.

"We must not stand idly by as our neighbors go
off to war. We must offer to help the families with
their work, caring for their fields, taking care of
their livestock. Families with sons and fathers who
are fighting will need our assistance, and we must
stand ready to help. Every person is our brother
and our sister and we must never forget that, even
though we may strenuously disagree with their
beliefs. Go forth in peace and do well."

Increase Joseph dropped his hands to his side
and bowed his head. The members of the
Standalone Fellowship quietly filed out of the
church. The lone robin continued to sing its spring
song.

The summer of 1861 went by almost normally.
The *Link Lake Gazette* continued to carry news of
the war's progress and Wisconsin's involvement.
A story in early May reported that President Lincoln issued a call for 40 regiments of volunteers
to serve for three years.

Wisconsin men volunteered by the thousands
that summer and fall. By the end of the year more
than 14,000 Wisconsin men volunteered to serve
in the Union Army. But at Link Lake, the
Standalone Fellowship farmers were tilling their
wheat fields, caring for their livestock, tending their
gardens and keeping a wary eye on war happenings.

In August an ad appeared in the *Link Lake Gazette* that caught many people's interest. "Your
man at war? Having trouble getting your wheat

fields harvested? We have the answer. The McCormick Reaper. It will cut your grain and gently place it in swaths. You need do no more than drive your team. Yes, women, if they can handle horses can operate a McCormick Reaper. Come for a demonstration at the John Henry Jones farm, two miles north of Willow River. Tuesday, August 15."

On that warm summer day, more than a hundred farmers from central Wisconsin gathered at the Jones farm, several of them members of the Standalone Fellowship. All were looking for an easier, less backbreaking way to harvest their grain fields.

Since the 1830s, farmers used cradles to cut their grain. The cradle was a one-person implement with a metal blade, a wooden frame, and a handle. Many men developed a rhythmic skill with a cradle, so that together with a helper who assembled the grain stems into bundles, the pair could cut and shock two or more acres per day.

With the war sucking manpower from the country, the number of men needed to cut the thousands of acres of wheat was vastly limited. Enter the reaper, which until this time had been ignored.

"Gather around," the McCormick salesman said. "Gather around and catch a glimpse at the future."

Increase Joseph and Henry Bakken at the last minute decided to drive their team down to the Jones farm, Henry to obtain a news story and Increase Joseph to see what all the fuss was about. They, along with their neighbors and many others, both men and women, gathered around a steel contraption to which a pair of fidgeting horses were hitched. The team was bothered by flies as they stamped their feet and swung their tails. The salesman didn't seem to notice their unease.

"Can you all see what stands here in front of me?" the salesman asked in a loud voice. He was wearing a white shirt with black suspenders that helped hold his trousers above his bulging middle. As he talked his red face got redder, and sweat dripped from his chin.

The crowd moved closer. The machine was different from what anyone had seen before. Everyone wondered how it could cut grain — they all knew how a cradle worked, but this fancy new machine, painted a bright red, bore no resemblance to a wooden handled cradle. It consisted of a metal platform with a strange scissors-like bar at the front, and a wooden reel with several wooden bars above. A steel wheel was located under the tongue where the horses were hitched.

"Stand back now," the red faced salesman announced. "Stand back. We'll show you how it works."

The man's assistant grabbed up the horses reins and said "giddup." He looked no more than a kid, maybe fifteen or sixteen years old, and skinny as a black locust fence post.

The team leaned into their harnesses and the reaper began to move. A loud clattering noise could be heard as the iron scissors bar, the salesman called it a sickle bar, began moving back and forth, clipping off the ripe wheat which the wooden reel knocked back on the wooden platform.

After moving a hundred yards or so, the red-faced man signaled for the boy to stop.

"Whoa," the boy said. The horses were already sweating profusely. The machine obviously pulled hard.

"Well folks, what do you think?" The red-faced man asked. "Have you ever seen anything like this? Are your muscles aching from using a cradle? No aches and pains when you own a McCormick reaper."

Once again the crowd gathered around the machine, kicking at the big iron bull wheel, feeling the wooden reel, examining the cut grain.

"I'm prepared to sell you a reaper today, special sales price for those who order right now. Those interested in learning more, line up right here and we'll give you the details."

The red-faced man's young assistant unhitched the team and led them to the shade of some oak trees that ran along one side of the huge wheat field.

Henry Bakken, Increase Joseph and much of the crowd of onlookers returned to their buggies. On the way back to Link Lake, Henry asked Increase Joseph what he thought about the new McCormick Reaper.

"Expect some of those farmers have no choice," Increase Joseph said quietly. Their men folk are off to war and the wheat has to be cut."

"Looks to me like the reaper will do the job, and easier, too," Bakken offered.

"I've got a concern, though," Increase Joseph said.

"And that would be?"

"The reaper is a machine."

"It is that."

"It's a machine that comes between the farmer and his land."

"Maybe a little," Bakken said.

"It seems a minor point, Henry, but more machines will follow. How does a person keep his love for the land if he can't be close to it, can't be directly involved with it?"

Henry was reminded of Increase Joseph's poor farming practices, how his crops were always planted late, how his harvesting came after everyone was finished — and how the reaper might help him. But he said nothing.

The duo was quiet for some time, the horses plodding slowly along the dusty road on this hot day in August. They passed a wheat field where two men were swinging their cradles, each one helped by a woman who gathered the wheat, tied it into bundles and stood them in shocks that were lining up across the long field.

"See those men, Henry. See how easily they swing their cradles. See the honest sweat on their brows and the smiles on their faces. See how they are one with the land, reaping the harvest. Notice how they move, to the beat of unheard music, back and forth, back and forth, almost effortlessly they work. And see the women, gathering the harvest. Gathering the ripe wheat into bundles."

"It's hard work," Henry said.

"Perhaps, but hard work builds character, gives people satisfaction, provides them with a sense of worth, a sense of importance, a sense of accomplishment. At day's end these men and women can look across this field and see what they've accomplished   It is there, in front of their eyes. What more could anyone ask?"

"You're right, I suspect."

"Look at me, Henry. I work day after day, trying to help people see the errors of their way, to point them in a new direction. Seldom do I know if I am accomplishing anything. But when I work on my farm, when I cradle grain, when I chop wood, when I plow with my oxen, I see the results of my efforts. And it feels good.

"Look at you, Henry. You don't know who reads your paper. You don't know if those who do read it understand what you've written. You are like me. We do our work, day after day, and we never know if it makes any difference. We never know. Want a drink of tonic?" Increase Joseph reached in his pocket for the ever present bottle and handed it to his friend who took a long drink.

"Tonic keeps getting better," Henry said. "Every batch is better." He handed the bottle back to Increase Joseph who drained it.

Chapter 21
War Troubles

July 1863

Increase Joseph and thirteen-year old Little Joe continued making the rounds with their sacred tent. People throughout the region learned about the teachings of this white-haired man in black from stories in the *Milwaukee Sentinel.* Substantial numbers of people didn't agree with him, especially the big land owners and even more so the fundamentalist preachers. But the sacred tent was usually full, standing room only. Everyone it seemed, whether they agreed with this spiritual leader or not, wanted to catch a glimpse of him and hear him preach.

Each week he set up his tent in a new community, and then stayed on for three and sometimes even four nights before returning to Link Lake to tend to his farm and replenish the supply of tonic. It would be a rare week that they didn't sell out the supply of tonic they carried.

But Increase Joseph was worried, not only about the war but about his father and mother back in Plum Falls, New York. Each year he wrote a letter to them at the end of the harvest season, where he reported in some detail on the activities of the Standalone Fellowship and their successes and challenges in Wisconsin. In early spring, usually in April, he got a reply from Plum Falls, an update on his parent's health (which had not been good in recent years), and a brief report of life in the community he left more than ten years earlier. He stopped by the Link Lake Post Office regularly inquiring about a letter from New York. But each time he received a curt, "No letter, Preacher Link."

Then, in early July, when he was walking by the Mercantile store where the post office was located, the postmaster beckoned him inside.

"This letter came for you yesterday," he said.

Increase Joseph didn't recognize the handwriting as he put the envelope in his pocket.

When he got back home, he slit open the envelope with his pocket knife and began reading.

"Dear Increase Joseph Link,

It is my sad duty to inform you that your father died on June 15 and shortly after the funeral your mother suffered a stroke and also passed away. The home farm has been sold. The receipts were used to pay your father's debts and funeral expenses for the two of them.

You have my deepest sympathies."

Sincerely,

Trutweiller T. Trutweiller, Attorney at Law

Increase Joseph dropped the paper to the floor and looked out the cabin window toward Link Lake. Tears began flowing down his face.

Meanwhile, the *Link Lake Gazette* carried weekly stories about the bloody Civil War, with details about the battles — Bull Run, the fight between the Merrimac and the Monitor in 1862, the mauling of Grant's army at Shiloh, and the battle of Antietam, the bloodiest single day of the war. Causalities on both sides mounted. Death and dying were constantly on Increase Joseph's mind.

All around Link Lake, men and boys marched off to war, with a few month's stop at Camp Randall in Madison where they trained, learned how to march, learned how to take orders, and left behind what they knew about logging and farming and small town storekeeping.

Of course everyone knew that the Standalone Fellowship members were at home, working their fields and trying to carry on normal lives. Most of the members stayed close to Link Lake, for if they traveled, even to Willow River, only fifteen miles away and someone recognized them as Standalones, they were called traitors, unpatriotic scum, lowlifes. Store keepers wouldn't sell to them, nobody would talk to them.

Link Lake itself had several storekeepers and a few residents who were not members of the Fellowship. Until the Civil War, they generally got along with each other. But now relationships were strained even between people who had lived and worked together for years.

Increase Joseph talked about this in his weekly sermons at the round church. He told people to be patient, that the war would soon be over and everything would return to normal. But the war went on with no end in sight. "No matter what," he told his followers, "we must not retaliate if our neighbors do not think well of us. They have a right to their beliefs, and we to ours." But life became difficult, increasingly so as the weeks and months passed.

Shortly after Andrew Blackwell's barn was filled with newly cut hay, it mysteriously burst into flames one night and burned to the ground, leaving behind a pile of brown ashes and some smoldering hay. The animals were all in night pasture, so they were not harmed. But the loss was nonetheless staggering. Some thought spontaneous combustion caused the fire, that Blackwell put the hay into the barn while it was too green. But he knew that was not the case. He told Increase Joseph that he was sure someone touched a flame to his barn.

"I sincerely hope that it is not so," Increase Joseph said. But he knew that it was probably true.

Fellowship members began staying up at night, watching their buildings and hoping their cabins or barns would not be next. As much as they were against violence, they sat up late into the night with their rifles at the ready, hoping against hope that they wouldn't have to use them.

Increase Joseph said in one of his Sunday sermons, "Misguided patriotism takes many forms, all too often violent. People mean well, but they let their emotions get in the way of common sense."

An explanation of what was happening did little to help those who were the targets of the violence.

One dark night, Adolph Lang was driving his buggy home from Link Lake, along the twisting lake road. Two men wearing masks jumped out from behind some trees, grabbed his horse by the bridle and dragged him off his buggy seat.

"Traitor," they yelled, as they beat him with their fists and kicked him unmercifully.

"Traitor," they continued yelling. They left him in the dusty road, unconscious, blood streaming

down his face and several ribs broken. Frederick
Henke found him the next morning, when he was
hauling grain to the mill. He quickly turned his
team around and took Lang to Increase Joseph.
After a half bottle of tonic and assistance from
Elwina Link, who had become not only a midwife
for the community, but someone who knew how
to attend cuts and bruises, Lang was on his way
back to his cabin. With a few days' rest, he was up
and about, but vowed he would not go to Link Lake
by himself.

So far, aside from sneers and off-color comments, Increase Joseph had been spared any violence or property damage. Until late February of
1863. Dog, that friendly animal with a generic
name that was so much a member of the Link family, came up missing. The family looked for him
everywhere. He was not in the barn nor in the
woodshed, his usual haunts.

Increase Joseph could not imagine that Dog had
run away, he was far too friendly and committed
to the family. It was also unlikely that he had gone
hunting, like some other dogs did. Dog was far
too much a homebody to venture out on an extended hunting foray.

As the Links sat at their kitchen table eating dinner, a knock came on their door. It was Henry
Bakken.

"I have bad news," he said. Increase Joseph
feared some more negative news about the war.

"I have found Dog."

"Thank goodness," Elwina said. Dog had been
her constant companion for many years. She especially appreciated his presence when Increase
Joseph and Little Joe were away with their tent

ministry.

"He's dead," Henry said. "He was lying in front of the newspaper office when I arrived this morning. He had a note tied around his neck."

"A note," Elwina said.

"It said, 'This is what happens to traitors.'"

"Where is he?" Elwina asked. She had begun to cry.

"The body has been mutilated," Henry said.

"I want to see it," Elwina said.

She rushed outside and found Dog lying in a pile of snow. His ears had been cut off and his eyes gouged out. The body with riddled with bullet holes.

"Oh, my God. My God," Elwina said. "Who would do this to Dog? He never hurt anyone."

Little Joe put his arm around his mother, trying to comfort her. Increase Joseph picked up the dog's body and took it to the barn. They would bury it when the ground thawed.

The *Link Lake Gazette*, in March 1863 carried the following story: "Men to be drafted. Local draft boards established to list men available for duty.'

Increase Joseph worried. He knew men from the Fellowship would probably appear on the draft list, and they would have to face the consequences of not going to war. And he was right. The bachelor brothers Joe and John Judd's names appeared at the top of the list posted outside the offices of the *Link Lake Gazette* in early July. The fellowship needed to make a decision. Increase Joseph first talked with Henry Bakken as to what they should do.

"Have you read the fine print about the draft?"

Henry said when they talked.

"Fine print?"

"Draft law says if a drafted man can find someone to take his place, or pay $300.00, then he is excused."

"We'll use the Tonic Helping Fund," Increase Joseph said. "We'll pay the $600 so the Judd boys can stay right with their beliefs. Take the money to the draft board, Henry. And have them cross the Judds off the list."

"I'll be on my way," Bakken said.

Meanwhile, Increase Joseph walked up the dusty lake trail to the Judd farm. He found the Judd boys sitting on their cabin porch, looking across their recently harvested hay field.

"Hello there, Preacher," Joe Judd called out when he saw the man in black approaching.

"I come with a message," Increase Joseph said.

"A message?"

"Your names are on the draft list," Increase Joseph said.

"We know it. And we are prepared to go. Ready to serve our country. To do our part." John Judd said.

"But it is against the Fellowship's beliefs."

"We are not afraid to serve. We have talked it over and we wanna go."

"You will not go to war," Increase Joseph said. "You will not take up arms against our brothers from the South."

"But it is our duty. President Lincoln says so. He says we must fight. All must be ready to fight."

"The fellowship has already paid the $600 so you don't have to fight. You are free to farm; you are free to follow the beliefs of the Fellowship."

The boys looked stunned. "Why did you do this? Now we must face the wrath of our neighbors. Someone will burn our barns. We'll be beaten, maybe killed if we stay."

"We will protect you," Increase Joseph said, as he turned and walked back down the trail. In his mind he hoped that the fellowship could protect each other, but it had become a great challenge.

Karl Smidmaier, Adoph's son was one of the first to be drafted. Smidmaier, not a member of the Standalone Fellowship, ran the livery stable in Link Lake, and since his unfortunate attempt to introduce malt water into the village, he had become quite successful, but not wealthy enough to offer $300 so his son could avoid war. He couldn't understand how the Fellowship members could oppose the war — he heard that the Judd boys were spared due to the Tonic Helping Fund and it made him furious. How could anyone, no matter what his religious beliefs, avoid the call of the President of the United States to serve?

On a hot July evening Increase Joseph heard a loud knock on his cabin door. He sat quietly by an open window, trying to enjoy the summer breeze that was blowing from across the lake, tempering some of the stifling summer heat that settled over the area. His mind never left the Civil War and all the death and dying that was occurring. If only there was something he could do.

Elwina went to the door. She recognized Adoph Smidmaier, even though his eyes were red and his deeply wrinkled face was a picture of agony.

"Mr. Smidmaier," she said. "Come in."

The big man bent down to enter the door.

"Josaph Link," he said in his heavy German accent.

"Yes," Increase Joseph said, as he stood and extended his hand.

"I not shake the hand of a traitor," he said in a voice that was near cracking.

"I got word about my boy," the big man said, his huge shoulders shaking.

"He is dead at place called Gettysburg. Shot dead. He come home no more."

"I am sorry," Increase Joseph said. "I am truly sorry."

"Your fault preacher man. Your fault. If Standalone men go to fight, my boy would be alive to help at livery with horses. He would be sitting at breakfast table. Singing as he worked. Karl a good boy. Happy boy. Always happy. And now he is dead."

Increase Joseph didn't answer. Smidmaier, in his profound grief, could not be responsible for his words or his tangled logic.

"I should hit you, bust your face," he said.

Increase Joseph stood in front of him, looking square at him and not saying a word. His hands were at his side, in one hand he held the Red Book.

"But hitting worthless man like you not bring Karl home. His blood is on your hands, Preacher Link. He died because of you."

The big man turned, hurried out the door and slammed it as he left, rattling the dishes in the cupboard.

"He's a good man," Increase Joseph said as he slumped back into his chair. "I wish I knew words of comfort for him."

He pulled the Red Book from his pocket and began paging through it. Elwina Link took off her apron, hung it on the hook by the fireplace and started down the trail to the Smidmaier's. She knew someone should be with Olga Smidmaier in her time of suffering."

It was well past midnight when she returned. Increase Joseph was still sitting by the open window, the Red Book in his lap. His eyes were red as if he had been crying.

"When will this war end, Elwina? It is tearing up our country, tearing up our communities. There is so much death. So much dying."

Increase Joseph stared out the window at the hot, black night.

"I must go for a walk," he said. "I must clear my mind of the agony that has penetrated it." He replaced the Red Book in his pocket, pulled on his black hat, kissed his wife on the cheek and left. He almost never kissed his wife.

Chapter 22
Vision Quest

July 1863

The following morning, Elwina saw that Increase Joseph had not returned. She awakened Little Joe and asked him to hurry down the trail to the Bakkens and tell them what happened.

Within the hour a search crew was organized to look for Increase Joseph. Henry Bakken feared the worst, that one of those who opposed the Standalone's position on the war found him and killed him. It was a daunting thought as the small search crew moved along the lake trail and then spread out into the woods. Periodically they called out, "Increase Joseph, Increase Joseph," but there was no response.

At nightfall, after a long hot day of looking, the small search party found no sign of Increase Joseph. Henry Bakken began wondering if he had been kidnapped and hauled away. Besides his enemies at home — the people who couldn't understand his anti-war stance — he also infuriated the basic Bible folks, and the well-to-do farmers. He said they were greedy and got their money by ignoring the land. Bakken was worried.

At daybreak the following morning, the search party was joined by a reluctant Sheriff Mortimer Evans from Willow River, the County Seat for Ames County. Evans, who fancied himself a Western sheriff, wore a wide-brimmed cowboy hat and cowboy boots with silver spurs that clinked when he walked. A big silver belt buckle was engulfed by his stomach, and a pearl-handled .45 pistol hung low on his right leg. His bushy white eyebrows shaded his eyes and made him look like he was peering out from a hairy overhang. His long white mustache hung down on either side of his mouth giving him a perpetually unhappy look. He rode a big bay horse.

"Well boys," he said in his gravely voice. A cigar stuck out from the side of his mouth.

"We're gonna find that preacher feller today. Never lost nobody yet that I didn't find. Sometimes we found 'em dead, sometimes we found 'em alive, but we always found 'em, one way or tauther."

Most of the search team was on foot, and all looked up at the sheriff wondering if his searching skills came anywhere close to his talk.

The sheriff pulled his pearl handled pistol from its holster, spun the cylinder, and pushed it back in place.

"Are you ready?"

Everyone nodded.

"Then let's get it done." He spurred the big bay in the ribs and the horse leaped ahead, galloping up the sandy lake trail, and leaving the search party in the dust.

Henry Bakken knew the sheriff since the Fellowship first arrived in Ames County. He'd heard the sheriff thought little of Increase Joseph, was likely pleased that he was missing and maybe dead. But the sheriff also knew it was his duty to help in the search, although it appeared that he was doing it by himself as the search party lost sight of him as he galloped up the trail.

The men fanned out as they did the previous day, once more walking through the woods at arms length from each other, looking in all the ravines, checking the brushy areas, but finding nothing. They assembled back in town at noon, and saw the sheriff's horse tied at the hitching post in front of the newspaper office. The sheriff was nowhere in sight.

Henry Bakken went in his office, and there sat Sheriff Evans, his feet propped up on a table. Abigail was working behind the counter, essentially ignoring the sheriff, who appeared to have been sleeping.

"Oh, Bakken, there you are," Evans said when he saw the newspaperman.

"Your men see anything?"

"Not a sign of him," Bakken said. "I'm worried that something awful has happened."

"Could be, could be," the sheriff said. He pulled his feet down from the table and stood up. "Like as not he had it comin'," the sheriff offered. "People don't like those that be different from them, those that run around sayin' stuff they don't wanna hear."

Henry Bakken didn't respond.

"You see any sign, Sheriff?" Bakken asked. He tried to control the anger that was building in his belly.

"Nope, searched high and low. Rode clear up ta end of the lake. No sign. Even asked a couple travelers on the rode if they'd saw a man in black. Said they didn't." The sheriff was looking out the window when he spoke, his back to the Bakkens.

Abigail whispered to her husband. "He's been sitting in that chair since ten this morning."

"'Spect he's long gone. You folks consider that he mightuv just run off? Vamoosed? Flew the coop? Left this place behind?"

"Not like him, Sheriff," Bakken said.

"Heard he was a bit on the strange order. Maybe runnin' off is what he did. You ought consider it."

Henry Bakken said nothing. He knew that the sheriff was going to be no help in their search for their spiritual leader.

"Tell you what I will do," the sheriff said. He turned from the window and scratched his layered belly. "I'll tell the sheriffs in Adams, Portage, Wood, and Marquette counties to keep an eye out for your missing preacher. Maybe one of them knows something."

"We'd appreciate it," Bakken said.

The sheriff tipped his hat to Abigail, walked out into the street and climbed on his big bay horse. He headed the horse south, on his way back to Willow River.

"No help there," Bakken said.

"Laziest man I ever met," Abigail offered. "Came in around ten, asked for some cold water, sat his fat behind down in that chair and hasn't moved all morning."

"I'm worried about Increase Joseph," Henry said. "He's been gone for two days. Somebody must have knocked him on the head and hauled him off."

"Talked with Elwina earlier this morning," Abigail said. "She's just worried sick. Little Joe wants to go out looking on his own, but she won't let him. Said it's just too dangerous these days. So much hatred around."

Bakken told the search crew to go home and get some rest that they'd give it another try later in the afternoon. Meanwhile, he decided to go up to the Links' and see if he could help with the chores. He found Elwina sitting in her rocking chair on the porch, working on her knitting. Her eyes were red and puffy; it was obvious she had been crying.

"Where's Little Joe?" Bakken asked.

"Out in the woods looking for his father. I couldn't keep him home. He's bound and determined to not stop until he finds him. Can't blame him really. I'm scared, Henry. These are terrible times. Why do so many people hate us?" Elwina asked, looking Henry Bakken in the eye. "Why, Henry? Why does it have to be this way?"

"I don't know, Elwina. I just don't know. Came to help with the barn chores."

"Thank you Henry, you are a good man."

Henry Bakken went out behind the cabin, past the well house and the small corn crib, past the log granary and the barnyard where the oxen and horses were resting to the two-story log barn. He pulled open the barn door and saw that the building was empty. He saw a small pile of hay, which he forked out in the barnyard for the animals. It was then that he heard the strange noise. It sounded like a hog grunting, but at the end of each grunt there was a low whistle, the kind of noise the wind makes when it whips around the corner of a building. Except this day there was no wind.

Henry stopped forking hay and listened intently. Nothing. Then he heard it again. The sound was coming from the second floor of the barn, from the hayloft. Henry climbed up the ladder to the upper reaches of the barn. Once upstairs, he stood quietly, waiting for his eyes to adjust to darkness. He brushed cobwebs from his face. And he listened. This time the grunting and whistling was much louder. He followed the sound to the far corner of the barn, behind a pile of freshly stored timothy hay. There was Increase Joseph, fast asleep. Empty bottles of tonic were strewn all around him.

"Increase Joseph," Henry said, shaking his shoulder. "Wake up. Wake up."

"Huh, huh," Increase Joseph responded. "What is it? What is it?"

"We couldn't find you, Increase Joseph. Everyone is worried."

"Worried. Worried. Why were you worried?

"Thought someone kidnapped you, or maybe killed you."

"Killed me?" Increase Joseph slowly sat up. He was holding his head. "Such a pain in my head. Such a pain." He had a heavy growth of white whiskers and his eyes appeared sunken in his head. His long white hair was tangled with timothy hay.

"What am I doing here?" Increase Joseph asked as he looked around. "Where is this place?" He pushed aside an empty tonic bottle.

"This is your barn, Increase Joseph. You are in your barn."

"My barn, my barn," the great spiritual leader looked confused. "Remember going for a walk a couple hours ago," Increase Joseph said.

"That was two days ago," Bakken said.

"Two days. Long time two days. Long time away," Increase Joseph said.

"What were you doing?" Bakken asked.

"On a vision quest. Trying to determine the future of the Fellowship. Searching for a message from God," Increase Joseph said. "A mighty vision quest it was. Bolts of blue lightning searing down from the heavens and entering my brain, giving me confidence and direction. God speaking to me, calming me, telling me to be patient. Saying I must not give up. Must not give up. Must not give up."

"I'm glad you're safe, Increase Joseph."

"Powerful dreams, Henry. Words from God. Messages about how we must never lose sight of the land."

"Can you stand up? Increase Joseph. I'll help you down the stairs." Increase Joseph wobbled to his feet, holding his head in his hands. The top of the Red Book stuck out of his back pocket.

"A powerful communication from God, Henry. Messages of caring. Messages of relationship and connections."

"Careful now, Increase Joseph. We're at the top of the steps."

"Powerful words, Henry. Words for many sermons. Words that will guide me for weeks to come."

"Here's the first step, Increase Joseph. I'll help you down."

Once at the bottom of the stairs, Henry Bakken helped support the man in black as they slowly walked toward the cabin. Elwina, when she saw them coming rushed out to embrace her husband.

"Powerful words," the man in black mumbled. "Powerful words."

"Come home, Little Joe," Elwina called toward the deep woods back of their cabin. "Come home, Little Joe, your father has returned."

Chapter 23
The Broadax Situation

October 1865

After his two-day "vision quest," Increase Joseph was back to his usual self, mostly. His mental state improved dramatically when he read the news that General Robert E. Lee surrendered to General Ulysses S. Grant at Appomattox Court House on April 9, 1865.

The very next Sunday, Increase Joseph delivered one of his most sobering sermons. Fellowship members arriving for the afternoon services came with smiles and celebration on their minds, as they all knew about the war's end, and even though none of their loved ones marched off to fight, many of their neighbors had.

Increase Joseph began, "We are gathered here this afternoon at a time that should be joyous, for the awful war that has struggled on for four years has finally ceased. We have learned about the freedom granted to our black brothers who lived in slavery their entire lives. For this we are thankful. But wars are never joyous. There is never cause for celebration, before, during and after bloodshed."

"Do you know how many Wisconsin boys are not coming home? Do you know how many of Wisconsin's young men, many of them still boys, were shot dead, died of disease, rotted in prisoner of war camps? Do you know how many?" Increase Joseph held the Red Book high over his head and his voice came near to rattling the windows of the round church.

"I have the numbers," Increase Joseph roared. "I know the carnage. Nearly 81,000 of our Wisconsin boys served in the Union Army. And . . ." he held the word. "And more than eleven thousand did not come home. Eleven thousand of our finest young men. Eleven thousand members of our future. Killed. Shot down. Struck down by disease. One in seven. One in seven who bravely marched off fell dead."

"And now we must begin the healing. Friends who became enemies must work at becoming friends again. It will be difficult, for old animosities are hard to overcome. But we must serve as examples. It is our God given mission. We must extend our hand to our non-Fellowship friends. We must extend the hand of friendship, for we are all God's people, no matter what our religious beliefs."

Increase Joseph sat down with his head in his hands. Members of the Fellowship quietly filed out the church. It was not the message they expected to hear.

The letter from Broadax, Wisconsin, arrived on a warm day in early October, 1868. The Civil War and all of its agonies was fading into memory. The letter was addressed, Editor, *Link Lake Gazette.*

Henry Bakken tore it open and read.

> *"Dear Fellow Editor:*
> *"I own and edit the* Broadax Crier. *Could you help me? Do you know of an itinerant preacher who always wears black and goes by the name of Rink, Dink, Link — something like that?*
> *"Olaf Larson, a cook in one of our logging camps, said he heard this preacher in a tent last summer. Olaf was quite impressed with this Rink, Dink, Link or whatever his name is and was wondering if I'd inquire about his coming up to the Northwoods with his tent. Olaf also mentioned the tonic he bought at the performance. He said it was the best medicine he'd come up against in some while.*
> *"If you know the whereabouts of this fellow, could you drop me a line ?*
> *"Much obliged,*
> *"Sadie Marks, Editor."*

Bakken shared the letter with Increase Joseph that afternoon. The preacher smiled, "They may not remember my name, but they never forget my message." He suggested Bakken write back offering some dates when Increase Joseph and Little Joe could go north to the great pinery.

Increase Joseph and Little Joe, who was 18, set out for the Northwoods with their wagons, sacred tent and many bottles of Link's Restorative Tonic. Little Joe closely resembled his father, except for the white hair of course. He was tall and slim with sharp facial features, a prominent nose and deep set eyes, and also wore black when they went on the road. His voice, which was always strong, had become even stronger. Increase Joseph considered giving him an opportunity to share the preaching one of these days. So far, Little Joe was content to sell tonic. His voice had such power that when he was home, he could call the Link's milk cows from the far pasture and avoid having to walk a half-mile to fetch them.

When he was selling tonic, Little Joseph sometimes equated that with calling cows. Except he was calling people, letting them know the wonderful virtues of this powerful elixir and cure for nearly all aliments. He knew he was also calling people to the sacred tent to hear the message from the Red Book.

The two wagons and their teams left Link Lake on a warm, sunny Friday in October, on their way to Broadax, located beyond Stevens Point a few miles, on the Little Eddie River that eventually flowed into the Wisconsin.

As the teams walked north, they left behind the wheat fields of central Wisconsin and entered the vast pine lands where lumbermen were slicing down the giant pines.

By Saturday noon they passed Stevens Point, a thriving sawmill town, and now traveled through a vast desert of pine stumps as far as they could see in every direction. They stopped to rest their horses and eat a cold lunch of Elwina's wheat bread sandwiches slathered with strawberry preserves.

"Not a pleasant sight," Little Joe said, as he looked across the vast expanse of pine stumps, many of them more than three feet across.

"Oh, the greed of some human beings. Wheat farmers with their vast acres. And now the lumbermen, who leave not a single tree, not one as their crews march across the landscape like locusts devouring everything in their path.

"Why did these lumbermen invite us? We cannot applaud these efforts," Little Joe said, as he looked across the expanse of nothingness. There was no bird song, no animals, nothing at all. A death scene. A scene similar to when a forest fire rampages across the land, destroying everything in its path.

"I fear the reactions we will receive from the people of Broadax," Increase Joseph said. "This could be a most challenging time for us, but we must forge on. It is our mission. We must confront those who seek to destroy the land and point out the error of their ways, and show them the road to recovery."

Increase Joseph and Little Joe approached the village of Broadax just as the sun was setting. The Indian summer sky was painted pink and red with streaks of purple, and the air hung heavy with the smell of pine trees. The huge trees around Broadax were mostly spared, at least for the time.

The town was small; Increase Joseph guessed it to be about three hundred people who lived in neat frame houses lined up along the Little Eddie River that tumbled through town with a fierce current.

As they drove down the dusty main street, they passed the livery and the mercantile store, and then drove by a string of small frame buildings, saloons with such names as The Naked Lady, The Shy Fox, Billy B's, Sally's Garter, the Jack Pine Tavern, and the Wolf Paw.

Lumberjacks were pouring into town, coming from every direction it seemed and beelining it for one of the drinking establishments. Almost all wore plaid shirts of various colors, mostly checks, wide suspenders, tall leather boots and floppy hats.

"Whoa," Increase Joseph said to his team. He stopped at the hitching rail in front of a little frame building with a false front and large window. The sign near the door said, "Broadax Crier." He tied up his team of tired horses.

Little Joe tied up his team as well and the two Links strode into the little newspaper office. A tiny, white haired woman, with a weather-wrinkled face looked up from a cluttered pigeonhole desk.

"Gentlemen, what can I do for you?" She said in an almost masculine voice. "I am Preach-er Increase Joseph Link," the man in black said, "And this is Increase Joseph Link II. We come at your request Madam."

"And I am pleased to see you. Mighty pleased. We don't see men of the cloth coming to these parts very often. She thrust out her hand and shook Increase Joseph's hand and then Little Joe's. My name's Sadie Marks. Just call me Sadie. Some folks around here call me Sad, but I prefer Sadie. Something about being called Sad doesn't seem right. Wouldn't you say?" She broke into a broad smile that split her face near in half.

"So pleased you're here. You know the history of this place?" Sadie scarcely took a breath between sentences.

"I don't," Increase Joseph said. He wanted to ask where he and Little Joe could put up their tent so they could start making preparations for the Sunday afternoon sermon. He opened his mouth, but before any words came out, she began spitting out the history of the town.

"It goes like this. At the beginning, we were just a little lumber camp here on the river. River had a long and wonderful Indian name that nobody from the camp as well as the Indians could pronounce. Well that logging camp had a woman cook. Some of the camps had women for cooks. Not many, but some of them did. Didn't make no matter to the lumberjacks whether the cook wore pants or a dress, as long as they could keep everybody's belly full with reasonable tasting grub."

Once more Increase Joseph started to ask about the location for their tent, but Sadie was intent on continuing her story. "This cook was a big woman. Arms as big as second growth popple trees. Name was Lena. Lena Ax. Appropriate name for somebody in a lumber camp, wouldn't you say?" She looked Increase Joseph in the eye, making sure he was paying attention.

"Nobody messed with Lena. She could flatten just about any lumberjack she came across, never heard that she did though. Men developed respect for her.

"Anyway, one of the men at the camp decided to name the village after her. Somebody suggested Lena, but that didn't seem like much of a town name. Someone else said 'Call the town Lena Ax.' Somehow that didn't seem right either.

"There wasn't much argument about her being big, especially across the back end. So some wise guy said, 'Let's call the town Broadax, that way it's named after Lena and at the same time after them big axes the cabin builders use. So after that the place was Broadax. Even Lena seemed kind of pleased that a bunch of rough and tumble lumberjacks would want to name a town after her."

"That's quite an interesting story, but Little Joe and I were wondering . . ." Sadie interrupted.

"Yep, I'll bet you're wondering how our river that runs through town got the name of Little Eddie? Well, the river had this long Indian name that nobody could pronounce so folks just got to calling it 'The River.' Worked fine for us here in town. When you got away from home and somebody asked about your town and you said it had 'The River,' they usually asked what was the name of the river. It seemed kind of foolish to say that it was just called 'River' like us folks didn't have enough sense to come up with a name for it.

"After that happened one too many times, town folks put their heads together one night in the Wolf Paw Tavern — that's the one just across the street there." Sadie pointed through the dusty window at a plain boarded building across the way.

"They met two or three nights trying to come up with an appropriate name for the river. A couple folks said we should go back to the Indian name, but that was voted down because not only couldn't folks pronounce it, no one had the first idea how to spell it.

"Finally, somebody remembered Eddie Kwaitkowski. He was this little Polish guy no more than five feet tall, but he was quick on his feet. Good dancer, too. Especially the polka. You should have seen him dance the polka. Girls would line up to leap around the dance floor with him.

"Well every spring the lumber companies floated their logs down the river. Sure as anything they'd jam up on the bend just south of town. When it happened, they'd call for Eddie

Kwaitkowski. He had no fear. He'd walk out on those floating logs in the river, like Jesus Christ himself. He'd poke loose the jam and get them big pine logs floatin' on their way again. One spring, he must have slipped or a stuck log broke lose and hit him. Nobody knows what happened. A fisherman found his body two miles down stream, caught on some bushes. Well that was the end of Eddie Kwaitkowski.

"We were wondering . . ." Increase Joseph broke in. But Sadie didn't even hear him. She'd stopped just long enough to draw a new breath.

"So someone said, 'Let's name the river the Kwaitkowski. Everyone agreed that it a good idea. But they soon discovered they had the same problem as before. Nobody could pronounce Kwaitkowski and fewer could spell it. So they were right back to when the river had the Indian name.

"I don't know who it was, but somebody said 'Nothing wrong with calling the river after Eddie's first name.' So they thought some on calling it the Edward River. Now Edward River sounded a little too highfalutin for a town called Broadax, so they finally come up with Little Eddie and that's what stuck. That's how the river got its name."

"We were wondering where to set up our tent," Increase Joseph said.

"Oh, I don't know anything about that. You'll have to ask Olaf Larson, he's the one to ask. It was his idea that you should come."

"Where do we find Olaf Larson?"

"Let's see, about this time a day on a Saturday you'll find Olaf across the street at the Wolf Paw. Place fills up on Saturday night. All the lumberjacks are in town wetting their whistles. Yup, you'll find Olaf over there. Good talking with you Preacher Link, always like to talk with folks from out of town. I learn so much."

Increase Joseph wondered what Sadie Marks learned from him. He had scarcely an opportunity to say his name.

Increase Joseph and Little Joe crossed the dusty street to the Wolf Paw. The man in black couldn't remember the last time he was in a tavern. As they approached the open door, they heard boisterous singing coming from inside, to the accompaniment of a loud piano. They stopped to listen.

We are tree cutters,
We men of the woods.
We live on baked beans and black tea.
We are tree cutters,
We men of the woods
We sleep with our axes, pick our teeth with pine branches, and keep bedbugs for pets yes siree.

Increase Joseph and Little Joe stepped inside the smelly room. It was like walking into the center of a forest fire because of the pipe smoke hanging in the air. The two men could scarcely see across the room. The place smelled like men who hadn't taken a bath in weeks, and who ate a heavy diet of baked beans.

Once they entered, everything stopped — the piano music, the loud singing, everything. All eyes were on the man in black and his companion.

Finally, the bartender piped up. "Looks like we got ourselves a visiting preacher." He was bald and had a dirty white apron tied around his middle.

"How can we help you preacher man? Assuming you don't want a drink of course." Loud laughter filled the room.

"You here to read from the Bible?" the bartender asked. More laughter.

"You gonna tell us what a bunch of sinners we are?" The laughter continued.

"I'm looking for Olaf Larson," Increase Joseph said. "I was directed to find him here."

"Olaf, you in need of a preacher? You plannin' on getting' hitched or something?" Loud laughter.

Olaf Larson, a huge man with a red beard and long red hair that came to his shoulders, edged his way through the crowd.

"You be Increase Joseph Link?" the big lumberjack asked.

"I am."

"Let's vee go outside to talk." The three men exited to the wooden sidewalk and walked a short distance away from the Wolf Paw. The loud singing continued. "We are tree cutters, we men in the woods. For Saturday night we all wait."

"Tanks for comin'," Olaf said. "Vee need your help. Vee need to hear your vords," the big Norwegian said. "Hear you one udder time, you have good vords. Good tonic, too." Olaf smiled. "Fixed up me sore back."

"We are happy to help if we can," Increase Joseph said. "Where should we set up our tent?"

"Got yust the place for you. Down by the Little Eddie. Down by the river there's a little field. Yust the right spot for your tent. You find it easy. Yust beyond the lumberyard."

"How will we get these lumberjacks to come to our meeting?" Increase Joseph asked. He was thinking about what he saw in the Wolf Paw and couldn't see that rowdy bunch sitting still listening to a preacher, no matter what he had to say.

"You yust leave that part ta me," Olaf said. "The men vill be dere. You say the time and they be dere."

"Four o'clock tomorrow afternoon," Increase Joseph said.

"Four it is, Preacher Link. The men be dere to hear your vords." Olaf shook Increase Joseph's hand and Little Joe's. He turned, walked back toward the open door of the Wolf Paw. Before he went inside he turned and waved. He had a big smile on his face.

Increase Joseph and Little Joe drove their teams to the field they spotted on the river, just north of the Broadax Lumber Company. They built a little campfire on the river bank and watched a line of thunder clouds building in the west. As they drank their tea the clouds rolled in and they felt the first splatter of rain. The thunder rolled down the river, tumbling over itself and mixing with the sound of the water pounding on the rocks a short distance from where the Links parked their wagons and tied their teams.

They crawled into their wagons and drifted off to sleep as the steady drum of raindrops beat on the canvas tops. The smell of wet pine needles drifted into the wagons, a pleasant contrast to the smells they encountered in the Wolf Paw Saloon.

As Increase Joseph drifted off to sleep, he wondered how many of these rough talking, hard living lumberjacks would stick their noses in the sacred tent. He dreamt that only two showed up, Olaf Larson, and little Eddie Kwaitkowski. He wondered how that could be since little Eddie was

dead. Maybe it was the ghost of little Eddie, coming by for a visit while Increase Joseph slept on
the banks of the river named after him.

Sunday morning dawned clear and crisp. The
storms clouds had moved away and a stiff breeze
blew from the West, rustling the tops of the big
white pines that surrounded the little field where
the Links camped. After taking care of their teams
and eating a light breakfast, the Links busied themselves with setting up the sacred tent, and erecting the folding bleacher seats. They had done it
many times before, and each knew what to do and
how to do it. They were finished in less than two
hours.

Little Joe positioned the tonic wagon in what
he considered the best location to attract sales,
and he put the tonic sign in place and piled the
boxes of tonic nearby at the ready.

Meanwhile, Increase Joseph, the Red Book in
hand, sat by the Little Eddie River, watching the
water flow by and glancing from time to time at
the pages of the sacred book. But mostly he looked
at the river, at the waters of the Little Eddie that
flowed clear and fast.

By three that afternoon the first lumberjacks
began arriving. Some looked a bit bleary eyed after their Saturday night carousing, but they were
a subdued lot, nothing like what the Links ob-
served the day before.

They lined up at the tonic wagon, at one point
the line stretched way beyond the sacred tent and
out into the field. Most bought two bottles, a few
three, almost no one bought just one bottle. The
reputation for the tonic has surely preceded the
arrival of the Links to Broadax. When there was

such strong interest in the tonic, Little Joe was always concerned that the men would buy their tonic
and leave, defeating the whole purpose of their
mission. But Little Joe saw not one man leave.
They politely purchased their tonic, stuffed it into
the pockets of their Mackinaw coats, and took a
seat in the sacred tent, waiting for the four o' clock
hour.

A few minutes before four, the tonic was gone.
Every last bottle. Little Joe packed twice as much
as they usually took on a trip like this, and it was
all gone. It was time for the sermon to begin. The
tent was full, standing room only. Except Increase
Joseph was not in sight.

After posting the "Sold Out" sign, Little Joe went
looking for him. First he looked in his wagon. Not
there. Then under the wagon. Not there. He
walked down to the river, and then he spotted him,
sitting with his back against a huge white pine that
stuck out over the river. He was fast asleep.

Little Joe nudged him awake.

"Did anybody show up?" Increase Joseph
asked. Rubbing his eyes.

"The tent is full to overflowing."

"Can't believe it. Can't believe it."

Increase Joseph brushed the pine needles from
his black coat and pants and strode into the sacred tent. A hushed silence came over the group
of lumberjacks.

Increase Joseph removed the Red Book from
his pocket, and held it with both hands as he looked
out over the rugged, bewhiskered faces of this
huge collection of lumberjacks. For what seemed
like an eternity, he said nothing. Someone said
later that a "sacred silence" moved over the group;

another wag reported, a "holy dread" overtook the woodcutters.

"Gentlemen and ladies," Increase Joseph began. Two or three women sat in the back of the tent, including Sadie Marks who had her notebook and pencil at the ready.

"I am deeply troubled, deeply troubled," the man in black said. A late autumn sun warmed the tent so the men dressed in their heavy wool shirts began to perspire.

"On our journey here, my son and I drove by hundreds of acres of cutover timber, only stumps remained. Only stumps. Nothing else. What a shame it is. What a disgrace to see these magnificent forests of the northland ruined. Decimated. Eliminated." Increase Joseph stopped for a moment to allow his words to settle in.

"It is not your fault. Not your fault that this is happening. You are told what to do. You are told to cut all the trees, every last one, even those that are not good for lumber. That is the message you are hearing. I do not blame you. You are good men. God loving men. You want to do right. But many of you believe you have no choice." He stopped again, and briefly found a page in the Red Book.

"It is all here in the Red Book. The words that give each of us direction in our lives, the words that keep us on the right track, that keep us in touch with the land, with each other and with God.

"You are God's creation, each and every one of you. And so are the trees and the creatures of the forest. All God's creations. God doesn't mind that you cut some trees. We all must work to make a living. God understands this. But God does not tolerate greed. Greed results in raping the forest, taking everything and leaving nothing. Greed destroys the land, and it destroys people as well."

Increase Joseph was warming to his topic, as his voice grew louder and louder, so was the temperature in the sacred tent warming. Perspiration was pouring off the faces of those lumberjacks sitting closest to the center of the tent, where no breeze from the outside reached. Yet, as they swabbed their sweating foreheads with big red kerchiefs, they continued listening. A strange sight it was, hundreds of red kerchiefs moving across the heads of lumberjacks, all listening intently to the man in black.

"The gold we are born with is the gold we leave with," Increase Joseph said in a voice that echoed through the tent. "We bring no wealth into this world when we are born, and take no wealth with us when we die. Yet, for so many men the accumulation of wealth is their sole goal in life — wheat farmers with large acreages, mine owners who move on when the ore is gone, and those who own the big lumber companies. It's a futile, misguided effort." He paused and stood silent for a moment. The lumberjacks red kerchiefs appeared as so many red flags waving in affirmation of his comments.

"But it need not continue. When your boss says, 'Cut all the trees,' ask him to reconsider. Tell him that it destroys the forest. You have a right to speak these words, indeed you have a responsibility."

The red kerchiefs continued moving.

"That's all I have to say." Increase Joseph held the Red Book high over his head and walked out of the tent, toward the big white pine tree on the edge of the Little Eddie River, where he was previously resting.

The lumberjacks walked into the cool autumn afternoon, not at all sure what they had heard, and what they should do about it.

"What'd that preacher man say?" one woodcutter asked his friend who had been sitting next to him.

"Wants us to tell the boss we shouldn't cut all the trees,"

"You tell the boss that, not me. I'm not gonna tell him."

Headlines spread across the first page of the *Broadax Crier,* "Preacher Says Save Some Trees. God doesn't want them all cut." Sadie Marks got a variety of comments from her readers, mostly negative. One of the most pointed came from a lumber owner, "Who the hell does this preacher think he is, telling us how we should run our lumber operations."

Chapter 24
Milk Cows

July 1870

"Warm day, Elwina," Abigail Bakken said by way of greeting as she spotted the pastor's wife working in her garden just beyond the Links' tidy log cabin. Abigail stopped by the Links' every week or so to talk with her friend.

"Getting dry, could use a good rain" Elwina said. The two of them explored Elwina's vegetable garden. They looked at the lettuce, peas, green beans, sweet corn, potatoes, cucumbers, beets, and cabbage. Elwina commented about each vegetable; she knew each plant and talked about it like it was a dear, dear friend.

"Look at the sweet corn, it is so green and tall this year. Little rain would help right now. And the rutabagas, oh how well they are growing. See these big rich leaves." She picked up one of the rutabaga leaves, exposing the purplish underside.

"Aren't rutabagas beautiful?" She said. "From the moment the first leaves poke out of the ground until I cook them and put them in a bowl in the middle of kitchen table. Increase Joseph favors rutabagas over about every other vegetable."

"Can't get Henry or Henrietta to even try them," Abigail said. "Don't even grow them in my garden anymore."

"Too bad," Elwina offered. "They are a fine vegetable and good for you, too. Good for the blood. Good for the digestion."

"You are starting to describe Link's Restorative Tonic," Abigail said.

Both women laughed.

"Come in the cabin," Elwina said. "I'm making a batch of cheese."

Upon entering the cabin, Abigail spotted a big kettle on the Links' recently purchased cook stove.

Most of the women in the Standalone Fellowship cared for the two or three cows each family owned. The women milked them, fed them, churned the butter and made cheese. Butter making was relatively easy — it meant skimming the cream from the top of the milk and then working the handle of the butter churn until butter formed, leaving behind sweet tasting buttermilk.

Cheese making was more difficult. You added rennet from a slaughtered calf's stomach to a kettle of milk, which made it curdle. You poured off the whey from the curds that formed. Then you pressed the curds into blocks removing the last of the whey. Most Standalone families made enough cheese for their own use, only occasionally did they have some extra, which they sold to the Mercantile store.

Elwina stirred the kettle of milk on her stove, pushing back a strand of gray hair.

"How is Increase Joseph these days?" Abigail asked.

"Working hard as ever. But I worry about him. He has these dark moments when he goes off by himself and doesn't talk to anyone. Sticks his nose in that Red Book and shuts out the rest of the world. I never mention it to him, just makes him angry. He says he's just fine. But I worry. He's starting to limp a little too. I think it goes back to when he was struck by lightning. Remember that time?"

"Think we all remember that," Abigail said. "Miracle that he lived."

"Lightning strike affected him more than we thought." Elwina said. "I know it did,"

"Anytime I can help, let me know," Abigail offered.

"You're a good friend, Abigail. A good friend. Some folks don't want anything to do with a preacher's wife. Glad you're not one of them." The two women stood quietly, Elwina occasionally stirring the kettle. The snapping and popping of the pinewood in the stove was the only sound in the kitchen, a special room the Links added to their modest log cabin two years ago.

"Henrietta still like working at the paper?" Elwina asked.

"She's a natural. Takes after her father. She's doing most of the writing now. Enjoys riding her horse through the countryside, looking for stories, searching for interesting people. She also likes those little sayings that people tell her. She picked up this one yesterday, 'Never say "whoa" in the midst of a hard pull.' Other words, when the going gets tough, don't stop," Abigail said.

"Liked the one in last week's paper, too," said Elwina. "Let's see how did it go? 'Beauty is often a splendid cloak which conceals the imperfections of the soul,'"

"Imagine, Elwina, both our kids are twenty years

old. Your Little Joe ever talk about Henrietta, ever mention her?"

"No, can't say that he has. But he's gone so much. Don't see him very often. He and his father are off on their tent mission about every week."

"Henrietta talks about Little Joe all the time. Says he's about the best looking fellow she's ever known. Says he's polite and smart. Even asked one day if he had a girl," Abilgail said.

Elwina laughed. "Those two have known each other since they were babies. The way they would pick on each other. Play tricks on each other. Wasn't that something?"

"Well these days, Henrietta gets this dreamy look in her eyes when she mentions Little Joe," Abigail said, smiling.

"About all that Little Joe seems to have on his mind is selling tonic and helping his father with their big red tent," Elwina said as she continued stirring the batch of curds and whey on her new shiny stove.

The following Sunday after church, Jacob Ornsby, Emil Groskeep, Andrew Blackwell and the Judd boys, Joe and John, motioned for Increase Joseph to join them under the shade of the big bur oak that grew just north of the Standalone Church. The hot and dry weather turned the once green grass around the church the color of dry straw. A light breeze blew off Link Lake, making it comfortable under the shade of the big oak.

Increase Joseph didn't know what to expect. He feared that something he said in his sermon rubbed these men the wrong way, and they wanted to talk with him about it. As his tent ministry gained a wide reputation, those who disagreed with his words slowly increased. Many people didn't want to hear that they had a responsibility to the land, they didn't want to hear Increase Joseph's ideas about farming, and forestry, and how they should avoid war and learn to get along with each other. Now Increase Joseph feared that some of this disagreement had settled into his band of followers, those who came with him from New York eighteen years ago to find a new life in the wilds of central Wisconsin.

"Increase Joseph," Andrew Blackwell began. "Have you noticed anything different about your wheat field this year?" Increase Joseph grew about five acres of wheat on his farm. He never quite got around to plowing more acreage, even with Little Joe there to help him. Father and son were gone too often to far flung places throughout the state, and even a time or two in nearby states — Minnesota, Iowa, Illinois and Upper Michigan. Elwina tried to keep the farm in order, but she couldn't do it by herself. Besides her summer chores, she also preserved many vegetables for winter use including dill pickles, apple sauce and sauerkraut, jams and jellies from wild grapes, wild plums, wild raspberries, and wild cranberries. Come fall, the cellar under their cabin overflowed with bins of potatoes and rutabagas, squash and pumpkins, plus all the preserved vegetables and fruits.

Elwina was also away often. She was either helping some young mother in childbirth, tending to injuries that were all too common — knife cuts, falls, kick from a horse — or sitting with those who experienced a loss such as the death of a loved one. The Link farm, beyond the garden, continued to languish. Members of the Fellowship often came by at critical times to help out, such as during haymaking or wheat harvesting. Several of the men, including those who wanted to talk with him, came by in early May and put a new roof on his barn. Some claimed Increase Joseph hadn't even seen that it was leaking. It was one of the Judd boys who said, "That Increase Joseph could be standin' out in pouring rain and he wouldn't know it unless you called it to his attention."

An inquiry about his wheat crop was about the last thing the man in black expected. "I haven't inspected my wheat lately," Increase Joseph answered.

"There's something wrong with it. Something terrible wrong with all our wheat," Andrew Blackwell said.

"What is the nature of the problem?" inquired Increase Joseph.

"It's dying. Our wheat is dying and it's not because of the dry weather," Emil Groskeep said. Groskeep grew about 20 acres of wheat in three or four fields, and each year his crop was outstanding; he hauled loads of wheat to the Link Lake Mill for grinding into flour.

"A little bug is chewing on the wheat stems, sucking the juice out of them so they dry up. Our wheat crop won't be half this year," Groskeep said.

"Let's look at my wheat field," Increase Joseph said. "It's just back of my barn."

The men walked the short distance to the field. The wheat heads were shrunken and misshapen, and the men immediately found the little juice-sucking bugs with black bodies and white wings with black triangular spots that were doing the damage. The little wheat destroying bugs were lined up on the wheat stems from top to bottom.

Hundreds of them. Thousands of them.

"Noticed the same thing near Willow River," John Judd said. "I was down there last week. I asked around. Got the same answer. Some bug has invaded the wheat fields for miles around.

Increase Joseph was shaking his head. He held several of the shrunken wheat heads in his hand.

"The land is talking back," he said. He waved his arms over his little wheat field. "It is telling us that planting wheat year after year is a mistake." He shifted into his sermon giving mode.

"We must learn to listen to the land. We too often miss the quiet messages, the little hints of action we should take. We should have listened earlier. We should have listened for the whispers when the land was reminding us of our ill-advised practices. Why do we avoid action until the land shouts at us as it does now? "

The longtime wheat farmers did not understand what their spiritual leader was saying. What whispers? What shouts? They wanted to know how they could save their wheat. They were little interested in messages from the land, no matter what form they took.

In that week's *Link Lake Gazette,* the bold headlines read, INSECT DESTROYING WHEAT CROP. The article continued. "An insect called the chinch bug has attacked thousands of acres of Wisconsin wheat, including the acres near Link Lake. There appears to be no remedy for the disastrous infestation. Wheat yields diminished by half."

Wherever people gathered, at the mill, at the Mercantile store, at the livery, the talk was about the failing wheat crop. Adolph Lang and Silas Stewart shared that they saw the bug in their crop last year, but it had done little damage. "I'll get a fourth the crop this year," Adolph Lang said.

No one knew what to do. The mill had a huge bin of wheat in storage from last year, and some farmers stored extra wheat as well. So there was no question that the Fellowship would have enough flour for its own use. But almost all the Fellowship farmers had become dependent on wheat sales for the money they needed to buy equipment and supplies, clothing and food—beyond what they were able to harvest from their gardens and obtain from their farm animals.

The following week, the *Link Lake Gazette* carried a story about milk cows and cheese making. Headlines were: MILK COWS REPLACING WHEAT.

The story was about Chester Hazen, a Fond du Lac County farmer, who had operated a cheese factory near Ladoga since 1864.

"Hazen cheese factory receiving the lacteal product of 1,000 cows for his cheese factory. Hazen is producing 16,000 pounds of cheese a month, some months more. He is shipping train carloads of cheese out of state, as far away as New York."

Now the talk in Link Lake switched from wheat growing to milking cows and cheesemaking. None of the men could understand how anyone could quit growing wheat and begin milking cows.

Silas Stewart seemed to carry the majority opinion, "Milking cows is women's work. No man should do it. Just ain't right. Men belong in the field, not milkin' cows in some smelly barn. We should never forget. There's women's work, and there's men's work. Big problems when you start messin' with that idea."

"Same with cheese makin'," Emil Groskeep chimed in. The wife makes the butter and the cheese in the kitchen. Don't understand what's going on over there in Fond du Lac County. What got into those men. They seem to have lost their backbone. Switching from doin' men's work to doin' women's chores."

The Link Lake womenfolk listened to the chatter and smiled.

Increase Joseph heard the discussion, too and read the various articles in the *Link Lake Gazette* and in the *Milwaukee Sentinel*. The *Link Lake Gazette* carried a brief story about the *Jefferson County Union* newspaper that a young man from New York State started on March 7, 1870. His name was William Dempster Hoard, and he was 34 years old.

The story reported how young Hoard, who was promoting dairy farming in southern Wisconsin, was using his newspaper as a way to help farmers understand what milking cows was all about.

"I must invite this man to Link Lake," Increase Joseph said. "The Standalone Fellowship must hear from William Dempster Hoard directly."

Three weeks later, when the Fellowship gathered at the Standalone Church on Sunday morning another man was standing next to their spiritual leader. He was tall, thin, had a prominent nose and a thick black moustache.

No one, absolutely no one ever shared the sermon pit with Increase Joseph. No one knew what to expect. Increase Joseph raised his hands high over his head, and immediately there was silence.

"We are faced with a great challenge." Increase Joseph began. People were wondering who this man was and what he had to say.

"The land has spoken to us," Increase Joseph continued. It has warned us that unless we cease growing wheat, our way of life may not survive.

We have seen the huge wheat fields to the south and west ravaged by the wind. We have seen the black clouds of dust roll over the landscape, tearing up the fragile wheat plants. And now, last year and this, we have seen the menace of the chinch bug that is sucking the life fluids from the wheat plant and leaving behind nothing but straw."

Increase Joseph lifted a handful of dried wheat stalks from the table next to him.

The visitor stood silent, staring straight ahead.

"Here is a man who has traveled a great distance. A man who has come from the southern region of our great state. A man who knows about dairy cows."

Emil Groskeep turned to his wife and whispered, "Dairy cows?"

"Shh!" she said. "Listen."

"His name is William Dempster Hoard, and like all of us, he, too, reigns from New York State."

"I am not a preacher," Hoard began. "I am a newspaperman."

The well-dressed man was a little nervous. He had spoken to many farmers about the virtues of dairy cows and cheesemaking, but was never invited to speak during a church service.

"We must say goodbye to King Wheat," he said. "And we must embrace the Queen, the dairy cow."

One of the older children in the back of church began to giggle. The idea of a scraggly, skinny cow as queen was beyond her comprehension.

"I have traveled around your community," Hoard said. "I saw your cows in your pastures. Poor looking cows. Good cows will earn you money, will replace the sale of wheat. But you need more than two or three, they must be of good quality, and you must feed them and house them during the long winter months. And you men must learn to care for them. You must do what your wives are doing now. Do not expect your women folk to do this work. Caring for cows will become men's work."

Several of the men looked stunned, like someone had hit them alongside the head with a two by four. Every woman was smiling.

"And men. You must treat your cows like the ladies they are." Smiles throughout the congregation. No one ever thought about their cows as ladies.

"When you cease plowing your land for wheat and turn some of it into cow pasture, the fertility will return and the soil will be restored. The winds do not blow away a cow pasture. The rains do not wash away pasture land. Cows will provide you with income and help the soil recover its fertility."

Increase Joseph stood to the side of Hoard, fingering the dried wheat plants.

"I will be in your community for a few days, residing with your pastor. I will come to your farm and show you what you must do to become a dairy farmer. I will help you understand why King Wheat has lost its throne and Queen Cow has replaced him."

Hoard sat down.

Increase Joseph, stood with his hands at his sides and his head down. "Let's pray," he said. "Thank you God for the wise words of this dairyman from the south. Thank you for sending him as a messenger in a time of our need. We will heed his words. We will savor his advice. Amen."

Usually the members of the congregation left the church in silence. This time there was chatter. The men especially wanted to talk with each other.

Knots of them gathered outside the church building.

Later, when it was time to do the evening milking, Increase Joseph said, "Tonight I will milk our cows."

Elwina smiled, but said nothing.

Increase Joseph found the milk pail and walked the path to their log barn where the cows were housed. Elwina had named them Sadie, Daisy, and Molly, but Increase Joseph didn't know which was which.

He grabbed the milk stool from its hook on the side of the wall and sat down under Sadie, or was it Daisy or Molly? The brown cow looked back at this unfamiliar person and lowed gently.

"I am to treat you like a lady," Increase Joseph said. He grabbed a teat with each hand and squeezed hard. He hadn't milked a cow since he left the farm in New York, and couldn't remember just how hard to squeeze. No milk squirted into the pail. He squeezed again, this time harder. Like an unseen weapon, the brown cow let fly with her back leg sending Increase Joseph, the milk pail, and the stool rolling in the straw. A barn cat sitting nearby ran for cover.

Increase Joseph picked himself up, brushed the straw from his black pants, gathered up the pail and stool and resumed the position.

"If I have offended you," Increase Joseph said to the brown cow, "Could you find a less violent way to inform me?" He and the cow exchanged glances. It was obvious that neither was comfortable with the other.

Before Increase Joseph got hold of the teats, the brown cow swung her wiry tail striking Increase Joseph in the mouth and almost knocked him over a second time. He remembered how to tuck the end of the tail into the bend of his knee. Once more, man and cow exchanged glances.

This time, Increase Joseph squeezed more gently and two slim streams of fresh milk zinged against the bottom of the pail. The cow stepped up and down a couple times, but did not kick as she had before. Increase Joseph continued, his hands rapidly tiring.

"I think I have regained my skill," Increase Joseph said to the cow and the barn cat. The cat also resumed its position, hoping for a squirt of fresh milk.

No more than seconds after the words left his mouth, the brown cow lifted up her manure covered back foot and placed it squarely in the middle of the quarter filled pail of milk. With great difficultly, Increase Joseph lifted the foot from the pail. He decided he had done enough milking. He took the pail of dirty milk to the house.

"You may want to strain this milk a couple additional times," Increase Joseph said. "Only milked one of the cows."

Elwina didn't even have to ask which one. She looked at him and smiled. She found another milk pail and hurried off to the barn.

Chapter 25
Fire At Peshtigo

September 1871

The 1871 wheat crop was as meager as 1870. The chinch bug cut the yields to a quarter of what the Standalone farmers had known in the 1860s. Several farmers started milking cows, even though the transition from wheat to cows was not easy. The biggest problem for men was moving past the belief that caring for cows was "women's work." Some Fellowship farmers absolutely refused to milk cows. The Judd boys, Joe and John, turned to raising sheep. They chided their cow-milking neighbors whenever they had a chance.

The Fellowship elders, shortly after Mr. Hoard's visit to their community, voted that the Tonic Helping Fund should be used to offer loans to those who wanted to buy cows and build more substantial barns to house them. Andrew Blackwell was the first to apply for a loan — $3,000. Next in line were Jacob Ornsby, Adolph Lang, and Silas Stewart, each for a similar amount. The Link Lake sawmill was busy much of the fall and winter, sawing out huge timbers, sometimes twelve inches square and thirty or more feet long to provide framing, and pine boards an inch thick, twelve inches wide and sixteen feet long to cover the outside of the new barns.

These Standalone farmers found another use for the stones they piled in the hedge rows surrounding their acres, and in huge stone piles in the middle of their fields. They brought in Welsh stone masons from the Pardeeville area, who built stone walls of many colors for their new barns.

Emil Groskeep, in addition to being a farmer, was a good carpenter, and it was he who supervised the barn building in the community. When each barn was ready to go up, the community held a barn raising, and everyone came to help — men, women, and children. The women put on a big dinner for everyone at noon. The men erected the huge wooden posts, hammered wooden pegs into the timbers to fasten them, nailed up the rafters and the roof boards, and hammered the sideboards in place. By day's end, what had been a new naked stone basement wall and a pile of lumber was now a beautiful dairy barn with a wooden cupola on the top.

Frederick Henke worked in a cheese factory before he moved with the Fellowship to Wisconsin. With a loan from the Tonic Helping Fund, he built a new cheese factory on the banks of Link Creek and not far from the grist and sawmill.

He was soon making some of the finest Cheddar cheese anyone in the community ever tasted. Henke named his product "Standalone Cheese." And it soon gathered a reputation that went far beyond Link Lake and the Standalone community.

For the first time, men were milking cows (some

of the women still helped them) but the wives no longer made cheese in their kitchens, although almost all continued to churn their own butter.

Increase Joseph convinced Henke to add a special room on to the cheese factory for the making and storage of the Restorative Tonic. For all these years, Elwina Link made the tonic in her kitchen, under the watchful eye of Increase Joseph, who would let no one see the recipe, not even Elwina. He would hand her the various ingredients, never identifying them and she would stir them into the bubbling concoction brewing on their wood stove.

Every couple months, Increase Joseph stopped by the Link Lake Cheese Factory and supervised the brewing of a new batch of tonic, allowing it to age in a dark room in back of the building. Since the day Increase Joseph learned from Kee-chee-new to add cranberries and maple sugar to the recipe, absolutely no one anywhere in their travels complained about the tonic. They kept the price the same (fifty cents a bottle, two for a dollar), but decreased the size of the bottles. Many bought at least two.

At one point, before granting loans for their newly emerging milk cow and cheese making industry, the Tonic Helping Fund had reached nearly twenty thousand dollars. Some tonic customers were critical, never about the tonic itself, but because they thought the money went directly to Increase Joseph Link. This was not true of course, and everyone in the Standalone Fellowship was well aware of the facts. Yet, snide comments from people outside the Fellowship often surfaced. "That man in black must be getting rich," was often heard.

Occasionally the words were spoken to his face. He didn't answer the complaints, but usually said, "The tonic will help you lead a better life." Increase Joseph was not one to defend his actions, or explain what he did and how he did it.

Henry Bakken once said, "Increase Joseph, you need more backbone. Some of these folks are walking all over you."

"Maybe so, Henry. Maybe so. But God works in mysterious ways. Sometimes you just have to be patient. Give Him a chance to work. Give Him a chance to work in His way, even if it is not in the way you'd like."

By this time of the year, Elwina's vegetable garden was usually a sight to see. The sweet corn would be shoulder high, the cucumber vines covered with green gherkins, the green beans flowering and yielding. But not this year. Starting in June the rains quit coming and the dry winds started blowing. Hay crops were poor, those who still grew wheat saw less crop than ever. Cow pastures were drying up. Cows were eating the leaves off low hanging tree branches.

A story in the *Link Lake Gazette*, now printed on a hand-driven Washington printing press that produced 150 one-sided pages in an hour, read, "FIRES IN THE PINERY. Dry weather and hot winds cause new fires to erupt nearly every day. Rain needed badly."

On some days, Increase Joseph noticed a smoky haze hanging to the north, and there were even days when the residents of Link Lake caught a whiff of smoke. But no one sensed any danger. A couple days of rain would snuff out even the worst fire, and surely rain would come soon.

On October 2nd, Increase Joseph received a letter from Luther B. Noyes, publisher of *The Marinette and Peshtigo Eagle*. In part the letter said, "Lingering small fires in our area are unnerving our citizens. The preachers, both those who are resident and those who have come in from the outside, haven't helped matters. Some of the preachers, especially those evangelicals from who knows where with their wild-eyed Bible thumping sermons are frightening the people out of their wits. One preacher said that the fires are God's wrath visited upon the people for their sins. We need a preacher who has a more level head. And from what I have heard of your work, you are the one. Could you come? I know you will get a crowd because our citizens are beside themselves with worry."

Increase Joseph immediately replied that he and Little Joe were on their way and would be there within a few days.

The two wagons, one heavily loaded with Link's Restorative Tonic, and the other containing the red sacred tent (another new round one that Increase Joseph just purchased), bleachers, poles, stakes, ropes and other equipment lumbered to the northeast. They turned north at New London, and traveled along the mighty Wolf River to Shawano, a sawmill town. They continued on to Oconto, another lumber town that received its charter in 1869. Here they had a chance to see the first steam powered sawmill in the region.

They drove along narrow, primitive roads that wound through thick stands of white pine and hardwoods— oak, maple, beech, ash, elm and white birch. In valleys, they encountered cedars, balsam fir and spruce. And everywhere there was smoke, although they saw no fires first hand. The smoke from distant fires hung especially thick in the valleys, and along the streams they crossed, where the wind had little opportunity to move it. At night, when the Links set up their camp, the sun set in an ominous sky streaked in red. And it rose each morning as a red ball that tried but always failed to burn through the smoke and smog.

When they finally arrived in Peshtigo on Saturday morning October 7, they saw small fires burning in the forests, flames racing along the ground, consuming dry leaves, and sending up bellowing, eye burning smoke. Bits of ash and soot were falling all around them, but the local people seemed not to notice as they tried to carry on their lives.

Newspaperman Noyes was walking down the street, his hat pulled low on his head, and a handkerchief held across his mouth. He was asking the lumberjacks and the farmers coming into town what they had heard and seen. The news was not good. Small fires were smoldering in all directions, not especially dangerous fires for when they came close to farm buildings, they were quite easily snuffed out. But no one thought to extinguish the fires entirely. Usually, in past years when a forest fire started, it was allowed to burn out, or heavy rains extinguished it.

Luther Noyes spotted the two canvas covered wagons rumbling into town, and read: "Preacher Increase Joseph Link. The Land Comes First" lettered on the first wagon.

Noyes ran up to the wagon.

"Whoa, whoa," Increase Joseph said to the team.

"Are you Preacher Increase Joseph Link?" Noyes asked.

"I am, and who might you be?"

"I'm Luther Noyes, the fellow who wrote you."

"This is a smoky place," Increase Joseph said, rubbing his smarting eyes.

"Get somewhat used to the smoke when it's here all the time," Noyes said.

"Saw several little fires in the forest just out of town," said Increase Joseph.

"Fires are all around us. Railroad crews mostly to blame. Cut wood to clear for the tracks. They stack up the wood and set it aflame, just to get rid of it. They don't care about the fire spreading as long as they can keep laying track."

"Another example of man fighting with the land," Increase Joseph said, shaking his head.

"Glad you're here. People need spiritual help. Too many believe this is God's work," Noyes said.

"I shall do my best to assist. Where might we erect the sacred tent?"

Increase Joseph was directed to a small open field near the river bank. When he and Little Joe arrived at the site, wood smoke hung just above the surface of the river, like ground fog in summer.

They set up their tent, put the tonic wagon into position and then decided to walk through town. Noyes said he would make sure that everyone knew they had arrived and that Increase Joseph would be speaking at 4 p.m. that afternoon.

"You that preacher man I heard was comin' to town?" an old man with a long white beard and wooden cane inquired.

"I am Preacher Increase Joseph Link," the man

in black answered. "And this is my able assistant, Joe Link."

"Missus and I are pleased you made it. Expect most other folks are, too. We need the help of the almighty. These infernal fires just keep on. Keep burnin'. Keep smokin' us like we was hams and bacon curin' in a smoke house."

"I shall do what I can, sir. I will do my best."

"You shouldav' been here a couple weeks ago. Town almost caught fire. Yes, it did. Was the 24th day of September, if I'm recallin' correctly. A Sunday it was. Fires been burnin' in the timber all around town. They was burnin' west of here, north of here, south of here, east of here — all round us." The man was swinging his arms in a big arc. "And then, on Saturday night all hell broke lose — pardon my words pastor."

"What happened?"

"Sparks and cinders jumped across the river, right over there. Them sparks landed on that pile of sawdust and dry slab wood, and commenced burnin' like nobody's business. Well, if they hadn't managed to snuff out the flames, this town wouldav' been a goner. Once they put out the fire at the sawmill, folks just gathered and watched the timber across the river burn. Nobody'd seen nothin' like it. Fire'd burn right to the top of a pine tree, creepin' out on each limb. It was the work of the devil. No doubt about it."

Increase Joseph wondered if newspaperman Noyes was right about his prediction that the sacred tent would be filled when the 4 o'clock hour rolled around. He and Little Joe returned to the wagons. Little Joe continued readying the tonic, while Increase Joseph retired to the covered wagon that carried their tent and was their living quarters while on the road. He studied the Red Book as intently as ever for the message from the land was as powerful here in Peshtigo as he ever heard. He had been a part of fierce wind storms that tore up the wheat fields. He had seen the forests in the north clear cut and devastated by greedy lumber barons. But never had he seen such fires and heard such stories of destruction, not only to the timber but to the wildlife that were caught in the fires — song birds, game birds, deer, bear. All consumed by the flames.

By three-thirty the sacred tent was filled with scores of people on the bleachers standing in the back. Tonic sales were brisk. People wondered if the tonic would help clear their lungs of the smoke, make breathing easier, and allow some soothing of their sore throats. Little Joe, trying to be honest, could only repeat what he repeated hundreds of times previous.

"LINKS RESTORATIVE TONIC. Settles a queasy stomach, calms excitable nerves, quiets an anxious colon, diminishes fever, controls worms, fights rheumatism, improves singing ability, helps to focus attention, makes unhappy people happy, shows the way for those who lack direction, represses headaches, toothaches and ear aches, makes one more attractive to the opposite sex and repels mosquitoes if used externally in sufficient quantity. Fifty cents per bottle. A dollar for two bottles."

No remedy previously helped. The people were willing to take a chance on the tonic.

Increase Joseph took his place in the middle of the tent, with people gathered all around. He stood with his hands at his side for a moment and then raised the Red Book high over his head. The only sound was the occasional cough from those suffering from the effects of the smoke.

"Ladies and Gentlemen," he began. Even his voice was a bit hoarse from the smoke-filled air.

"I am here to help you in your hour of need, to give you solace in a time when the very hinges of hell are evident in our midst. The forests are burning, sending up clouds of black, throat choking, eye watering smoke." So far he said nothing that everyone in the crowd did not already know, and know well.

"Some of you are wondering. Is this God's doing? Is God punishing you for your sins? Is the wrath of God upon you? And if it is God's wrath, what have you done to deserve such treatment? What awful deeds have you done to evoke such a terrible response?" Increase Joseph put his hands in front of him, clutching the Red Book tightly. He said nothing, looking out over the collection of faces dirty with soot.

He stood up tall, pulled back his shoulders, and spoke in a voice that some later said sounded like the voice of God himself.

"These fires are not your fault. God is not punishing you. God is a loving God, a caring God, an understanding God. So why are these fires all around you, burning valuable timber, killing wild animals, sending wild birds scurrying for their lives?"

He stopped again for emphasis, and drank a swallow of tonic that he had previously poured in a glass that stood beside him.

"Those who own the railroads, they are the ones

who deserve blame. They have tampered with the
naturalness of the land, they cut the timber to
make room for the iron rails and they pile the
wood high and set it aflame. Blame them, the railroad owners. It is not God's doing. It is the work
of men, money hungry men who are not listening
to what the land is telling them. We all suffer for
the deeds of the few who live miles from here, in
elegant homes with fine food and servants."

Once more he raised the Red Book high above
his head. "This book has the answer. It contains
the word to follow in hard times and in good. When
you cut all the trees and burn them, the land talks
back. At first quietly, in messages you may not
hear. And then in a way that will get your attention."

Everyone sat spellbound, listening to words that
were different from those of other itinerant preachers who came to Peshtigo, waved their Bibles and
proclaimed that the fires were God's payment to
the dammed.

"Oh, how difficult our lives are. The lives of
the poor and hardworking. The lives of those trying to make a living where the challenges are many,
the sacrifices are considerable and the returns
slight. And then, to add to the discomfort, we must
often live with the consequences of the uncaring.

"When people misuse the land we all pay. Rich
and poor. Guilty and innocent." Increase Joseph
stopped for a moment and looked out over the
vast crowd of red-eyed, coughing people.

"God gives us the strength to confront situa-
tions that make our lives miserable and unreward-
ing. He will not intervene. It is up to us to take
action and makes things right."

Increase Joseph, his voice extremely hoarse was nearly exhausted.

"God is with you," Increase Joseph said. His eyes were smarting from the smoke. "He is not against you. He is not judging you. He is not punishing you. It is not his way." Increase Joseph sat down and began coughing. The tent was soon empty as people left to face the unknown of the days ahead.

The late afternoon sky was a crimson red and the soot and ash continued to fall. People of the village went to bed, except for the most committed drinkers at the Peshtigo House who continued rabble rousing into the depths of the night.

Sunday morning was a continuation of the previous day, except the sky, like a giant hand, began to push down on the residents of the area, making it even more difficult for the people to breathe than in previous days. The parched marshes several miles south had been burning for weeks, and the noxious fumes from the smoldering muck drifted into town on a southwest wind that began to pick up as the day progressed. The temperature slowly rose. About two hundred men arrived that Sunday morning to work on the railroad, and they were whooping it up in the tavern, mostly oblivious to what was going on outside.

Increase Joseph and Little Joe decided to take down the sacred tent and pack it away. "Too much soot and ash in the air," Increase Joseph said. "A live ember may fall on the tent and catch it afire. We'll do our afternoon sermon outside."

The two men, wiping their stinging eyes, worked slowly as it was impossible to draw a lungful of fresh air.

"Maybe we should leave town," said Little Joe.

"These people need us; they need the soothing words of the Red Book in their hour of need. We cannot leave."

Their teams were stamping their feet, and throwing their heads in the air, considerably agitated.

"Something bad is going on," Little Joe said. "Look at the horses."

"Animals often know before we humans when something awful is to happen," his father answered.

"What can be worse than this?" asked Little Joe.

"I don't know. I don't know," said Increase Joseph as he tucked the last tent stake into the wagon and tried to wipe the sting from his eyes.

Many residents of Peshtigo, sensing an even greater calamity than they already experienced, began digging trenches in the dry soil, and burying their valuables.

"Maybe we should bury some of our tonic," said Little Joe.

"No, we will do nothing to show our fear of what might come our way," said Increase Joseph.

By late afternoon, the wind became a gale and thunder boomed in the distance. The sky was a menacing red, with huge clouds hanging like the udders of milk cows.

Without further warning the tornado struck the town, carrying on the wind the tongues of flame that devoured everything in its path. People began running toward the Peshtigo River, their only hope for survival; the wicked wind and searing flames tearing at them, propelling them.

The air was filled with cinders, dust and the all

consuming flames.

Increase Joseph and Little Joe watched as the holocaust struck the town, setting building upon building afire. One moment the structure was standing in the smoke, the next moment it was totally engulfed in flame.

"What will we do?" Little Joe asked. A look of panic on his face.

"We must help these poor people," Increase Joseph said. We must try to help them."

A young woman with her long hair on fire ran past, stumbled and fell. Soon her entire body was burning. The awful smell of burning flesh drifted toward the Links.

The sawmill, not far from where the Links located their tent, was burning fiercely. The air was filled with the sounds of horror — horses screaming as they burned and died, Men and women calling for each other, searching in the smoke, little children yelling in terror.

A man driving a team pulling a wagon with his wife and children in the back raced for the river. As the Links watched, a huge ball of fire landed in the wagon setting everyone in it on fire. The man continued driving, urged the horses to run ever faster, not knowing that his family was perishing, that his mission was futile.

Increase Joseph watched as the bridge crossing the river caught on fire and then collapsed sending hundreds of people plummeting into the water below. People from both sides of the river erroneously assumed that the other side was safer.

"We must go to the river," Little Joe said. "Or we too shall perish." Little Joe untied the horses so they were free to run for the river, too.

"I must remain. I must help where I can," said Increase Joseph.

"You cannot help; we must save ourselves,"

"I cannot leave them. I cannot run away." Increase Joseph said.

Little Joe never before disobeyed his father, but with a giant shove, he pushed the man in black into the river and jumped in behind him.

Increase Joseph's head bobbed to the surface and Little Joe swam up beside him. What appeared to be a whiskey barrel was floating in the river, stuck behind a giant rock. Little Joe saw the barrel first. "Grab hold," he instructed his father.

Together the men held tightly to the barrel, at least they were temporarily safe. People were plunging into the river all around them. A young man was sobbing uncontrollably and speaking gibberish.

"How can I help," said Increase Joseph.

"There is no help," the man said. "My wife is dead. Burned. I carried her to safety, but when I got in the water, it was not her. It was another woman. And she is also dead."

The man grabbed a hunk of wooden bridge work and floated on downstream. Just then there was an explosion in the direction of the Links' wagons, which were engulfed in flame. Then another explosion and still another.

"The tonic," said Little Joe. "The tonic is blowing up."

Each explosion sent a plume of fire into the air, like Fourth of July fireworks. "Bang, woosh. Bang, woosh." The exploding tonic — blue, yellow, purple flames — lit up that entire side of the river, in the midst of the firestorm that was consuming everything and everyone in its path. Horses and cows were floating everywhere in the river, bumping into people.

"So cold," Increase Joseph said. "I'm so cold." They had been in the chilled river water a couple hours, and though the fire was still raging on shore, the water temperature was taking its toll. Little Joe moved around the whiskey barrel and put his free arm around his Father. "Pray to God," Little Joe said.

A tall, thin man, no doubt also feeling the cold, walked from the river up on the bank—and immediately burst into flame and died.

"I am about to meet my maker," said Increase Joseph, as he relaxed his hold on the whiskey barrel.

"You must hold on," Little Joe said. "People need you."

Increase Joseph struggled to hold the barrel. His teeth were chattering and his face was turning blue.

A woman floated by the Links, grasping the horn of a frantic milk cow. "It is the end of the world. It is the end of the world," she repeated again and again.

Sometime before dawn the worst of the conflagration passed, and those who survived began emerging from the river, shivering and calling for their loved ones. "Sadie, Sadie," an older man called. "John, where are you John?" a sallow faced woman screamed.

The village of Peshtigo was no more. Hunks of molten metal, bent horseshoes, metal wagon rims were seen here and there. The buildings were gone. Huge timbers that had been a part of the wooden tub factory smoldered. Piles of iron circles that held wooden tubs and buckets together lay in the rubble. A dead man lay face down, his head encircled by one of the iron rims.

Little Joe emerged from the river, carrying his cold and nearly blind father. Little Joe could scarcely see either because of the smoke and soot in his eyes had been exposed to all night. They followed the small band of survivors who trailed toward a little valley by the river's edge, which was sheltered by sand hills. The little valley had been spared, even the small trees and shrubs that grew there.

Some of survivors in this little untouched valley of life attended the sermon the previous afternoon and recognized Increase Joseph. He was sitting up and drinking some hot tea that someone prepared. His color was returning to his face, but he was coughing. A woman offered him some tonic, from a bottle she had purchased from the tonic wagon the previous day. He took a long drink.

"Do you have a few words for us Preacher Link," another women asked.

Increase Joseph tried to stand, but was unable to do so. In a voice that was little more than a loud whisper he said, "Many of you have lost family; several of you are yourself hurt. You have lost your homes, your horses, your cattle. But God will help you recover from your loss. God is a caring . . ." Increase Joseph did not finish the sentence. He slumped to the ground, having fainted.

Little Joe rushed to his side. Someone offered a drink of water. Most of the day, Increase Joseph was in and out of consciousness. Little Joe stayed by his side, caring for his father. Several horses survived the fire in the river, including two that belonged to the Links. The other two, along with the wagons, tents, seats, and tonic all perished.

By the following day, Increase Joseph regained enough strength to ride one of the horses, and the two of them set out for home, Little Joe leading the way. It was a long arduous journey, with many stops so Increase Joseph could rest. It wasn't until they got home that they learned about the Chicago fire, which killed 300 people on the same night the Peshtigo fire took 1,200.

Chapter 26
Increase Joseph Recovers

April 1872

I ncrease Joseph did not recover quickly from Peshtigo fire injuries. Upon his return to Link Lake he took to his bed. Even with daily self-prescribed doses of the Restorative Tonic and Elwina's loving care, by mid-April he was not yet able to preach to the Standalone Fellowship on Sunday afternoons.

As was the policy of the Standalones, anyone had the right and indeed was encouraged to stand before the Fellowship and speak. Almost every Sunday someone filled the breach, with only a few exceptions. Even when no one stood to speak, the Fellowship felt the presence of God all around them in the silence of the round church as they sat for most of an hour, thinking and reflecting, each in his own way.

To the surprise of some, Henrietta Bakken, the tall, blue-eyed daughter of the newspaper editor, with hair the color of wheat straw, stood and offered words that she later printed in the family newspaper.

One Sunday she spoke for nearly an hour on

the simple phrase: "When the road is smooth and the way is clear, hold tight to the reins."

She spoke with a strong confident voice, and although not everyone captured the meaning of her message in the depth she had intended, many members came to her and told her how much they appreciated her thoughts. Some members, who never expected a woman to address them, especially one so young, were most surprised with the depth of her wisdom.

Two weeks later Henrietta spoke again. With a strong but pleasing voice, she began:

"The land is a place to celebrate and a place to mourn.

"A place to laugh and a place to weep.

"A place to work and a place to play.

"It is forever the same, yet always changing.

"It reminds us of yesterday, helps us celebrate today and points us toward tomorrow."

There were more laudatory comments. How had this young beauty become so insightful and so poetic? The words she spoke were the thoughts of Increase Joseph, but spoken in a new way, with a careful woman's touch.

Little Joe never before heard Henrietta speak before a crowd. He enjoyed her writings in the *Link Lake Gazette*, but he was even more impressed when she delivered them in person. Little Joe, perhaps more than anyone else in the Fellowship, suddenly noticed how she looked up with her deep blue eyes for emphasis, how she used her graceful hands to make a point subtly, yet forcefully. How she allowed her sometimes melodious voice to rise and then fall, like the waves that lapped the shores of Link Lake. He began to see her in a new way, not just the little girl he teased as a child.

After her second talk, he went to thank her and tell her how much he enjoyed what she said, and especially the way she said it. But when her blue eyes looked into his, he couldn't think of a word to say, not one.

He stood dumbstruck, and she just smiled before she took one of his hands in hers and said "Thank you for being here, Little Joe." The touch of her warm hand on his sent a shiver through him that he had never before known. He opened his mouth to speak, but no words came.

"I need some advice," she said. "Would you meet me by the lake in a little while? I want you to read something that I wrote for the newspaper."

"Sure, sure . . ." Little Joe stammered.

Later the two were seen walking along the shores of Link Lake as the warm spring sun was setting across the water. It appeared that Henrietta was doing all the talking.

Another Sunday, Jacob Ornsby, who twenty years earlier stood up and proclaimed his dislike for mosquitoes, took the opportunity to return to the theme that apparently was still on his mind.

"I wish to once more take this opportunity to talk about God's big mistake. Creating the blood sucking, sleep preventing, skin stinging mosquito. I know deep in his bosom, God must know that creating mosquitoes was a blunder. But why, after all these years, why hasn't he done something about them? Rid the country of them! Send them into oblivion, or at least move them to Willow River.

Emil Groskeep whispered to his wife, "I think Willow River has all the mosquitoes they want."

She smiled.

The audience sat attentive, respecting the rights of anyone who felt the urge to speak. Some were smiling, as Jacob, in all seriousness, went on talking about God's greatest error. Most couldn't wait until he finished, wondering if he would make an even a bigger fool of himself as he went on, describing in great, tedious detail his various encounters with mosquitoes, including some of the tall tales he'd heard.

"Lumberjack told me that a horde of giant, Minnesota size mosquitoes invaded his lumber camp one spring. The men ran for cover under a big bobsled that was used for hauling logs. What saved them was this. When the mosquitoes drilled their stingers through the bottom of the bobsled — two inch planks they were — the men bent the stingers over with hammers. Problem now was tryin' to keep those big mosquitoes from flyin' off with the bobsled. Took all the strength of the lumberjacks to keep the bobsled on the ground. The sound of all them mosquito wings beatin', trying to lift up that bobsled was like the worst kind of windstorm. Wind from the mosquito wings did tear most of the tarpaper roof off the cookhouse."

Now there were broad smiles all around. Finally, Jacob sat down and the Fellowship filed out of the church, chuckling about Jacob's mosquito sermon.

Another Sunday, Adolph Lang stood up and began extolling the virtues of the milk cow.

"Like the lady she is, the milk cow is a wondrous creature. Not only a thing of beauty, she gives up her milk so that we may have cheese and butter, and cream on our strawberries.

"Have you ever looked into the big brown eyes of a milk cow? If you haven't you should. She never talks back, never grumbles, never complains. Oh, the milk cow, what a lady."

Adolph was saying all this with a most serious look on his face. The Fellowship didn't know if he was serious, or trying to have a little fun. They didn't know if they should smile, or seriously consider what he was saying.

As the Fellowship filed out of the church that Sunday afternoon, the big question on everyone's mind was, "Was Adolph serious?" Most everyone remembered when Adolph Lang and most of the rest of the Fellowship was dead set against cows and caring for them.

One of the Judd boys was heard to mumble to the other: "If Adolph Lang can brag about his cows, then we ought have the right to go on about the virtues of raising sheep."

Little Joe decided it was time to get the Fellowship back on track. It was true that everyone had the right to say what he pleased, but shouldn't the church be more than a discussion of mosquitoes, cows, and sheep?

The following Sunday, Little Joe, took his place in front of the Standalone Fellowship. He wanted to be true to his father's teachings, yet he wanted to share his own thoughts as well. He chose as the title for his talk, "Go to the Woods."

Little Joe, tall and thin like his father, had a voice that was even deeper and carried further than the famous spiritual leader's.

He began with a report on his father's condition. "The Preacher Increase Joseph Link, my father, will stand before you and share his message within a few weeks. He is out of bed and taking short walks each day. He has regained much of his voice. Thanks to the power of the Restorative Tonic and your prayers, our spiritual leader is on the mend."

There was a thunderous round of applause. It was what everyone wanted to hear.

"Today, I want to fill in as best I can for my father," said Little Joe. He looked ever so much like his father when he was preaching, except there was no Red Book. The Red Book survived the dunking in the Peshtigo River, but it still remained in Increase Joseph's pocket. Absolutely no one had an opportunity to page through it and learn about its profound message.

Little Joe began, in a voice that carried to every nook and cranny of the round church, "Go to the woods," he said. "Go to the woods to see the beginning and the ending of life — the newest seedlings and the fallen, dead trees.

"Go to the woods to dream, to rid yourself of your burdens and refresh your soul.

"Go to the woods for comfort, for inspiration, for knowledge.

"Go to the woods to see God's creatures living in harmony with each other — the oaks and the maples, the aspen and the pine, the deer and the fox, the owl and the hawk.

"Go to the woods to see beauty in the ordinary, feel the joy that comes from simple things, gain pleasure from the commonplace.

"Go to the woods to gain a sense of who you are, in this place, at this time.

"Go to the woods alone, seeking solitude and the opportunity to clear your mind of everyday living and its problems.

"Go to the woods to discover the deeper reaches of your being.

"Go to the woods in winter, when the trees are naked, the snow is piled high and the only sound is the wind playing with the bare branches.

"Go to the woods in summer, when everything is green and growing, where bird song is everywhere and the trees provide shade and comfort to those who seek it.

"Go to the woods to rid yourself of the dictates of others who would tell you what to believe and what to do.

"Go to the woods to discover yourself as you become acquainted with God's wondrous works.

"But above all, go to the woods."

Little Joe's comments were well received. Nearly everyone said that it gave them something to think about, and that they would never see a woods in quite the same way.

Henrietta Bakken was last to speak to Little Joe.

"Your words were beautiful, Joe, absolutely beautiful. You are a poet," she said. He fumbled with his hands and blushed.

Chapter 27
The Marriage of Little Joe
June 1876

I t had been a long time since there was such
excitement in Link Lake. Saturday, June 17
was the marriage date for Increase Joseph
Link, II and Henrietta Bakken. No one could understand why it took them so long to make up their
minds about marriage. They were both 26, well
beyond the age when most young people in Link
Lake wed. They were often seen talking together,
walking along Link Lake and attending various
social functions in Link Lake. The rumor spread
that if the decision had been Henrietta's alone, the
knot would have been tied several years earlier.
But she was persistent and patient. Henrietta was
well aware of Little Joe's shyness, perhaps more
so than anyone else. Even though he was bright,
had many good ideas, and was an excellent
speaker, when alone with someone, especially a
woman, he could scarcely find his tongue. But he
had gotten better or so said Henrietta one time
when her mother inquired if Little Joe ever said
anything when they were together.

People wondered if Little Joe found enough
words to ask Henrietta to marry him or if Henrietta,

quite a headstrong young woman, had simply taken the bull by the horns and did the asking. It became a topic of discussion at the Link Lake Mill, at the Mercantile store and at the cheese factory where farmers regularly gathered. Folks agreed that she probably asked Little Joe regularly, and within the last month or so had finally gotten a response from him. Of course no one would ever know the truth of the matter. Like his father, Little Joe sometimes got confused about such things as social events, and probably his own wedding. The Judd brothers firmly believed that Little Joe may have said yes to marriage, but believed he was answering quite a different question, such as do you like apple pie? When talk of the marriage moved through the community, more than one person reported that Little Joe, as he wandered around town, looked more confused than ever.

John Judd met Little Joe on the board sidewalk outside the Mercantile store in early June.

"Hear you're gettin' hitched?" Judd asked.

"What, what . . . What did you say?" Little Joe replied. His mind seemed to be some other place when he was out walking.

"Hear you're gettin' married?" Judd repeated.

"I must go," Little Joe said. "The woods beckon." Either he still hadn't heard what John Judd had asked, or he simply couldn't accept what he and Henrietta had agreed to do.

Henrietta on the other hand, was bouncing around town with a big smile on her face and a friendly, "How do" to everyone she met.

It was Jacob Ornsby who brought up the topic of the upcoming marriage one day at the cheese factory. "No question about whose gonna wear the pants in that marriage," Ornsby said, laughing.

"Sure like to be a mouse in the corner on their wedding night," Silas Stewart offered. "I don't think that boy knows the first thing about what he's expected to do."

"We'll all find out soon enough," Jacob Ornsby said.

Aside from what all people were saying and thinking, the wedding was scheduled for Saturday, June 17. The ceremony itself would be performed by Increase Joseph in the Standalone Church. Following the ceremony everyone in the community, whether Standalone members or not, was invited to a reception in the sacred tent, erected just north of the church.

Increase Joseph Link, recovered from his bout with the Peshtigo Fire and a night in the cold river, was back to his old self, mostly. But he was no longer the vigorous young man he once was. At age fifty, he walked a bit stooped, he tired more easily and his limp had become more prominent. The only after-effect from his winter-long illness after the fire, was a persistent cough that sometimes prevented him from speaking as long as he wanted.

He sat on the porch of his modest cabin the Friday evening before the wedding, watching the sun set across Link Lake and thinking about his ministry in Wisconsin and about his family, Elwina and Little Joe who were always there to help him.

He thought about how Little Joe, when just a young boy, took to selling tonic like a professional. He remembered all the trips they made around Wisconsin, and beyond, to the lumber camps, to the little farming communities, to the larger towns. Most of the tent meetings were highly successful, but some were less so. He remembered the time when the wheat farmers asked him to pray for rain, and when he chastised them for planting such large fields that the wind had free sweep, they threatened to burn his tent. He recalled the terrible years of the Civil War, when Little Joe was still a youngster. He remembered the lumberjacks in Broadax and the polite reception he and Little Joe had gotten, even when he blamed the lumber barons for raping the land. And how could he forget Little Joe saving his life when they plunged into the Peshtigo River and watched the village burn.

As he was sitting quietly, glancing now and then at some pages in the Red Book, Elwina joined him. Since Increase Joseph's illness, Elwina regularly found time to be with Increase Joseph, even though few words passed between them.

"I've been thinking about Little Joe and Henrietta," Elwina said, when she sat down beside him on the well swept and worn porch.

No response from Increase Joseph, who closed the Red Book and looked off toward the lake.

"Remember what a good job Little Joe did the Sundays when he preached for you?" She asked.

Increase Joseph shook his head in agreement.

"Remember his sermon on going to the woods, and how everyone thought it was wonderful?"

Another nod of agreement.

"And isn't that Henrietta Bakken just about the most wonderful woman any man could ever hope to have as a wife?"

No response from Increase Joseph.

Both Little Joe and Henrietta continued to give occasional Sunday sermons, at the request of the Fellowship who said they didn't want Increase Joseph to over extend himself. The truth of the matter was, they appreciated the fresh ideas these two young people brought to the Fellowship, and they enjoyed their lively ways of presentation.

Emil Groskeep was heard to say, "That Little Joe sounds just like his father did ten years ago."

No one would say beyond hints such as Groskeep's that Increase Joseph's speaking style had diminished some over the years. Yet no one ever questioned the power of his ideas and the strength of his convictions about the land and how important it was in the lives of everyone.

"Do you remember how well people liked Henrietta's talk a few weeks ago? She started with a simple idea. She talked about the words, 'Do the best you can with what you have.' That's all there was to it. One sentence and she had everyone sitting on the edge of their seats as she spelled out how important it was for people to work hard knowing we all have limits."

"Yes," Increase Joseph said.

"We can't do as much as we once did," Elwina said. She was thinking about Henrietta's words, and about her husband, the man in black who believed he could work as hard as ever, and then was disappointed when he discovered he couldn't.

"So much yet to do," Increase Joseph said. "So much yet to do."

"Time for bed, Increase Joseph," Elwina said. "You have a big day tomorrow."

"I need some time alone," Increase Joseph said. "I'll be in shortly."

A mosquito buzzed around his head and he smiled as he thought about Jacob Orsnby's extended treatise on the mosquito as God's biggest mistake.

His thoughts took him back to his only son. He

wondered if Little Joe would continue in his footsteps and take over the Standalone ministry, or if this strong minded young newspaper woman would lead him in another direction.

He also thought how different it would be not having Little Joe living in their cabin, ready to help out with the barn chores, ready to help Elwina when she needed help in the house.

Little Joe and Henrietta planned to live in a little cabin on a small farm about a half mile from Increase Joseph's, a cabin that several of the Fellowship members helped build. As Increase Joseph continued thinking about his only son, tears welled in his eyes. Finally he got up from the porch, rubbed his eyes, stretched and went into the cabin. A lone kerosene lamp stood on the middle of the kitchen table. Elwina had already gone to bed.

Saturday dawned clear and cool. A light breeze blew from the southwest, riffling the surface of Link Lake. A robin called from high in the big oak tree near the Standalone Church.

Increase Joseph was up early as was Little Joe. Together they did the barn chores, milked their five cows and turned them out to pasture. Little Joe fed their small flock of chickens, usually his mother's chore, but this day he volunteered to do it. Increase Joseph made up a gruel of ground oats and corn and mixed it in a pail before dumping the pleasant smelling mixture in the trough for the pigs.

When the chores were done, the two men filed into the cabin where Elwina prepared a breakfast of hotcakes with butter and maple syrup — Little Joe's favorite food.

The wedding was scheduled for 1 p.m. Everything was ready. Henry and Abigail Bakken and some of their friends decorated the church with wildflowers that they picked in the meadow near the lake.

The Standalone Study Circle — after a futile start several years ago they had renewed their effort and met regularly — decorated the sacred tent to be used for the reception with pine bows and white ribbons. Not only did the tent smell like a pine forest, it looked beautiful as well. The Study Circle women had also been cooking and baking most of the week, so no one attending the reception would go hungry.

After breakfast, Little Joe said he was going for a walk by the lake. Increase Joseph went to his study to prepare the remarks he would make at his son's wedding ceremony.

Elwina busied herself around the cabin, cleaning and tidying up in case Increase Joseph might invite some of those attending the wedding to the cabin.

"Where is Little Joe?" Elwina asked when she prepared a light lunch.

"Said he wanted to walk by the lake," Increase Joseph answered.

"He should eat and pull on his wedding clothes."

Increase Joseph finished a bowl of Elwina's tomato soup, and then pulled on his best preaching clothes.

"Should we tell someone to go looking for Little Joe," Elwina said. She fidgeted with a strand of gray hair that fell over her eye.

"He'll be here shortly," Increase Joseph said. "I will make my way to the church. I have to make preparations."

But Little Joe did not return. Elwina hurried up

the trail that connected their farm with Blackwells'. Andrew and Mabel were just about to leave for the church.

"Have you seen Little Joe?" Elwina said.

"No, can't say as we have."

"Said he was going to walk by the lake, and we haven't seen him since," Elwina said. "He'll be late for his own wedding."

"You and Mabel go on to the church," Andrew said. "I'll go find him."

Andrew Blackwell hurried down to the lake, only about a half mile from his farm and walked along the lake path. There, under a big tree, he found Little Joe fast asleep.

"Wake up, Little Joe, you'll be late for the wedding," Andrew said.

"Wedding, wedding, what wedding?" Little Joe said, stumbling to his feet and brushing the grass and leaves from his dirty barn pants.

"Your wedding."

"My wedding?"

Andrew Blackwell grabbed Little Joe by the arm and hurried him along the path to the road, and then up the hill to the church. The churchyard was parked full of horses and buggies.

Blackwell and Little Joe, who wore pants soiled with cow manure and a torn dirty work shirt with two buttons missing, made their way to the front of the church where Henrietta Bakken, her father, and Increase Joseph stood waiting.

It was clear that Henrietta, who was dressed in a beautiful white gown with a garland of wild daisies on her head, had been crying. Henry Bakken, usually quite an affable fellow, had a look that would kill. Little Joe, still under the control of Andrew Blackwell, stood in front of his father, who looked him over from top to bottom.

"Come with me," Increase Joseph said. He led his son to the little preacher's room in the back of the church.

"Here," Increase Joseph said. He handed his son a bottle of the tonic.

"Take a big drink of this."

Little Joe had been selling the tonic for years, extolling its virtues, but not once had he even tasted the magic elixir. He took the bottle, lifted it to his lips and drained half of it. He rubbed his hand across his mouth, blinked a couple times, and handed the bottle back. Increase Joseph drained the bottle and father and son returned to the marriage ceremony.

The ceremony itself went well, at least that's what folks later reported. Little Joe had to be prompted twice to say, "I do," but he managed finally to spit out the words in such a quiet whisper that Henrietta could scarcely hear them.

Finally, Increase Joseph said, "I pronounce you man and wife."

He scarcely uttered the words, when Henrietta grabbed hold of him and kissed him hard on the lips. The women in the audience gasped for they had never before seen such a public display of affection. Little Joe's knees buckled, but Henrietta held him tight so he couldn't fall. His manure stained trousers tangled with the folds of her lily white dress.

For what seemed like an eternity to some of the more pious members of the Fellowship, the two embraced — or rather, Henrietta embraced Little Joe. Then the two of them walked briskly down the aisle toward the outside door. Henrietta had a big smile on her face, Little Joe looked confused, like he had no idea what just happened.

Everyone adjourned to the sacred tent for food and refreshments. There was a huge bowl of lemonade. One of the young men of the Fellowship who worked at the cheese factory snuck away to the tonic storage room back of the cheese factory and borrowed a couple dozen bottles of the Restorative Tonic. He dumped all of it into the lemonade and took the empty bottles back to the cheese factory so no one would be the wiser.

Many people attending the wedding reception said they never had a better time. To a person, everyone praised the lemonade and asked the Circle ladies who made it for the recipe. For weeks the Mercantile Store could not keep lemons in stock. Everyone followed the Circle recipe, but no one came close to replicating the taste of the lemonade at the Bakken-Link wedding. Some even accused the Circle women of leaving something out of the recipe they shared. They claimed on the authority of the Red Book itself that they had not.

To quell all rumors of Little Joe's ineptness in matters involving marriage, nine months to the day of the wedding, Increase Joseph III made his appearance in the world. Still, one disbeliever maintained it was all Henrietta's doing. No matter. Someone quickly named the baby boy, Little Joe Too.

Chapter 28
Problems With Progress

August 1884

"How are you, Increase Joseph?" said Henry Bakken when he greeted his old friend.

Henry walked up the hill from his newspaper office in Link Lake to the Links' cabin, just down the road from the Standalone Church. It was a warm afternoon, with scarcely a breeze rustling the leaves of the big nearby oak trees. Increase Joseph was sitting on his porch, as he often did these days, looking out across Link Lake to the west, and the lush farm fields of his neighbors to the north.

"Not good, Henry. Not good," Increase Joseph replied. "I'm worried."

"You're always worried," the newspaperman replied. Look at you. You've got a comfortable cabin, a good wife, a son and daughter-in-law that help you all the time, and the cutest grandson in Link Lake." Of course Little Joe Too was also Bakken's grandson.

"I know, I know," said Increase Joseph. "It's all the changes that I'm worried about. It is so easy to forget about the land."

"Change can be good," said Bakken. "Look at me. I have a new printing press. I can turn out newspapers twice as fast as before. With our new Sholes and Glidden Type Writer we don't have to write in longhand. Typewriter was invented over in Milwaukee you know, by a guy name of Christopher Sholes. Came up with the idea in '68."

Bakken wondered if the great preacher even heard what he said.

"Been thinking about our town, Henry, and all the people who have moved in. Most of them have nothing to do with our church — they ignore it. Happy to have us buy goods in their stores, though. Started two more churches — Lutheran and Methodist."

"You've forgotten the fifteen couples who've joined our Fellowship. These people believe in you, Increase Joseph, and your message about God, People and the Land."

"Maybe so, Maybe so," the great preacher mumbled. "Walked down Main Street the other day. Tell you what I saw," the man in black continued. "I saw many new businesses."

"They're not all new. Some have been here twenty years."

"I remember when Main Street had only the Roberts Mercantile Store, Smidmaier's livery stable, Karl Kempen's barber shop, Jones furniture and undertaking, and your newspaper office. That was it. Now look what's there. Do we need all those businesses?"

"Our town is growing, Increase Joseph. The state is growing."

"Moving too fast, Henry. It's growing too fast. I

listed all the establishments on Main Street — too many to remember anymore." He glanced at a sheet of paper where he scratched some notes.

"There's John J. Jones, Clothier and Hatter; Johnson Brothers, Farm Tools; and O. B. Brewer, M.D. In the early days we didn't need a doctor in town. Then there's E. B. Ryan, Watches and Jewelry. Why do we need a watch and jewelry store? Then you come to I. P. Gillett, Dentist who claims he'll pull your teeth without pain if you ask. A. C. Strong has a place where he sells plows, cultivators, harrows, and hay rakes. There's the Link Lake Pump and Well Company. Remember when we helped each other dig wells, Henry? Now we got a fellow in town who'll do it. And would you believe it, we've got a lawyer, John Joseph Evans is his name. Do we need a lawyer?"

Henry Bakken knew all of this, of course, because Abigail sold advertising to these people regularly, and their money helped Bakken increase the size of his newspaper until it was the biggest and most important in Ames County.

To chide his old friend, Henry added, "Don't forget, Increase Joseph, now you can order just about anything you want, from kerosene lamps to a new shirt from the Montgomery Ward Catalog."

"I know, I know. All the ways that we can spend our money."

"Hear you're putting up the sacred tent at the Ames County Fair this year," said Henry Bakken.

"It was Little Joe's doing. He made the arrangements. Not so sure it's a good idea. Folks coming to the fair aren't interested in my message. Some may want to buy a bottle or two of tonic. Tonic always sells."

Two weeks later, Increase Joseph and Little Joe loaded up their wagons and made the short trip to Willow River, the site of the Ames County Fair. They put up the sacred tent in the far corner of the fairgrounds, near a lineup of new farm machinery that sat ready for inspection by fairgoers. The following day the fair opened. Families from miles around drove their teams to the fairgrounds for a glimpse of the horses, cattle, hogs, and sheep on exhibit. They saw grain and hay samples on display, fancy quilts and sewing that were to be judged and of course the new machinery.

The first tent show sermon was scheduled for 3 p.m. the first day of the fair, with another set for 7 in the evening. During the morning, the Links walked around the fairgrounds, inspecting the various exhibits.

Little Joe was most attracted to the machinery exhibit, especially to the J. I. Case Threshing Machine that was powered by a big Case steam engine. The threshing machine threshed grain for fifteen minutes, every hour on the hour. The Links along with fifty or more farmers stood in the hot sun waiting for the next demonstration.

Promptly at 1 o'clock a bearded man wearing a straw hat, bib overalls, and a red handkerchief around his neck, climbed onto the back of the steam engine. He pulled a rope and the steam whistle screamed, causing the audience to jump for most had not been this close to a steam engine before.

He then pushed some levers, and the long leather belt that tied the steam engine to the threshing machine by means of big pulleys began to move, slowly at first and then more rapidly. The threshing machine, an implement as large as a small building, with pulleys and belts moving in every direction, began to shake and shudder as the steam engine got up speed.

The engineer on the steam engine motioned to the men standing on a wagon load of oat grain to begin tossing bundles onto a chain driven elevator that dragged the oat bundles into the mouth of the machine, where they disappeared from sight.

Soon, yellow oat straw spewed out the huge pipe on the back of the machine, creating a cloud of dust. A man stood at a spout on one side of the machine, where a canvas bag collected the grain that was separated from the straw.

"Sure easier than pounding the kernels out of the grain with a flail," Little Joe said.

"But look at the size of that thing," said Increase Joseph. "And the noise. How can anyone work with that noise?"

A huge cloud of black smoke belched from the stack of the steam engine as it labored to keep the threshing machine moving and at the proper speed.

"And the dust and the smell," Increase Joseph added. "Who would ever want one of these contraptions?"

"Threshing machines and steam engines are the future," said Little Joe. Someone told me there are already a dozen of these big machines working in Ames County, going from farm to farm threshing grain. Look how much easier it is, and so much faster, too."

"Little Joe, tell me this. Why do people want to do things faster, all the time faster? What has happened to doing things more slowly, more deliberately so they can enjoy the work and have time to contemplate the gifts that the land has given? Working around that threshing machine you don't have time to enjoy anything. That machine controls you. Look at those men tossing bundles into it. They have no time to stop. No time to talk. No time to think. The machine keeps beckoning them to throw in more bundles."

"Father, it's progress. It's one way to make farm life easier."

"But just because it is easier may not make it better. I wonder if people are thinking about that, taking time to consider what they are doing when they ask these machines to do their work."

"I don't know, father. But we cannot stand in the path of progress."

They walked on and looked at McCormick's new grain binder that not only cut the grain but tied the grain into bundles, all in one operation.

"Heard that the binder's new twine bundle knotter was invented right here in Wisconsin," said Little Joe. "Fellow's name was John Appleby. A person doesn't need to run behind the reaper and gather up the grain bundles and tie them anymore. Appleby's invention does it. Ties bundles automatically."

They walked by an enormous plow that turned three furrows at the same time and was pulled by a steam engine, the same kind that was powering the threshing machine.

They stopped to look at a new steel windmill that was turning in the breeze, and scarcely making a noise. Most of the farmers in Ames County owned windmills, but wooden ones that pumped water from wells sometimes two hundred feet deep.

"Not much to break on this steel windmill, weather won't destroy it either, like it does with the wooden ones," Little Joe said. His father didn't answer.

Now they came to a display of barbed wire. Three strands of it enclosed a small area, next to which was a similar sized area enclosed with a wooden fence, the type that many farmers still used. A sign read, "Joseph Glidden Barbed Wire. Guaranteed to keep your animals where you want them to be."

But for Little Joe, the most interesting demonstration of all was the new telephone that was on display in the exhibit hall. A telephone set was on one end of the building and another on the opposite end. People could talk to each other with their voices traveling over a thin copper wire that connected the two devices.

"Give it a try," a man dressed in a white shirt said.

"Don't think so," said Increase Joseph.

"What's it do?" asked Little Joe, more than a little curious.

"You can talk to somebody miles away. Voice travels over this wire." The man held out a thin copper wire for Little Joe to touch. "Everybody will have one. Gonna replace the telegraph."

Little Joe pondered the last statement. Now, besides sending a letter to someone, which took days and sometimes weeks to arrive, a person could send a telegram. But to do that, they had to travel to a train depot. The nearest train depots were in Berlin and in Plainfield, where railroads passed. It was a long horseback ride to either place from Link Lake.

"Telegraph works well," said Little Joe.

"Telephone will replace it. Mark my words," the man in the white shirt said.

Increase Joseph was staring off in space, while his son and the telephone man talked, apparently oblivious to what they were discussing. Slowly father and son walked back to the sacred tent, where Increase Joseph climbed into his wagon and began studying the Red Book in preparation for his afternoon presentation.

As expected, people began lining up at the tonic wagon shortly after 2. Much to the surprise of Little Joe, the tent was three-quarters filled by two-thirty and standing room only at 3, the appointed hour. Little Joe was so busy selling tonic, he hadn't looked around for his father. He closed up the tonic wagon promptly at 3 and walked over to the wagon.

"Father, it's time," he said quietly as he approached the tent. But his father was not in the tent. Frantically, Little Joe looked under the wagon, but no Increase Joseph.

The piercing whistle of the steam engine powering the threshing machine split the air, signaling that the 3 o'clock demonstration was about to begin. He glanced in that direction, and saw his father standing in the back of the small crowd watching the threshing machine come up to speed.

"Father, it's time," Little Joe said as he ran up to the man in black. Oat chaff was gathering on the shoulders of his coat.

"It's you, Little Joe," said the great preacher. "How can I be of assistance?"

"It's time for your talk. The tent is filled."

"The tent is filled?" Increase Joseph said. His

wrinkled face looked confused.

"The people are waiting for your message."

"I have a message?"

"Yes, father. They are waiting. Come quickly."

The young man and his aging father hurried to the tent, where people were patiently waiting to hear from this great spiritual leader who spoke of things beyond what most heard from their own pastors. Just before he entered the tent, he took a quick drink of tonic, and found the Red Book tucked deep in one of his pockets.

As he arrived in the tent, a huge ovation went up from the crowd. This was surely more than he expected in the way of welcome.

He brushed some of the oat chaff off his coat, lifted his arms high overhead, and began.

"Ladies and gentlemen" he said. His voice was not as strong as it once was, but loud enough to overcome the sound of the steam engine and threshing machine operating not far away.

"I am privileged to speak with you today. To bring you words from the land and from God, for these messages intermingle and are one." He stopped briefly to glance at the Red Book.

"I am pleased to be a visitor at this great county fair. I commend you for coming. But I am also troubled." Once again he paused, and drank from a glass on the little table standing next to him.

"The theme of this great fair is 'Progress in the '80s.' A chance for you to see the newest farm machinery, the finest farm animals, the most up-to-date appliances for your home — cook stoves, fancy kerosene lanterns, cistern pumps, fancy furniture. You can see steel windmills, and even barbed wire fence to enclose your animals. Some of you have already seen a new machine that allows you to talk to people a distance away, with your voice traveling over a thin copper wire. All of this is called progress." Once again he stopped. The inside of the tent was warming as the hot August sun beat down on it. Increase Joseph removed a red handkerchief from his pocket and swabbed it across his forehead.

"But I have problem with progress." he said in a voice loud enough to be heard well beyond the sacred tent.

"In our zeal for change, in our great interest in things new, in our love for innovation, we are ignoring basic truths. We are forgetting that we are all of the land, tied to it directly now and forever more. As we buy new machines, steam engines, big plows, huge harrows, and horse drawn discs that we can ride, we are losing our contact with the land. We treat the land like another machine." He paused once more for emphasis.

"When we act like the land is a machine, ignoring it as a living thing, the land rebels. I have seen it happen. I have seen the wind blow away the wheat fields. I have seen the nothingness that remained when the northern woods were clear cut. I have seen wild fire devour everything in its path.

"The land nourishes us as we must in turn nourish it. As we sever our connections with the land, through the use of machines, through ignoring the messages the land sends us, we are disconnecting ourselves from our souls."

Once more Increase Joseph paused. He was sweating profusely and his left hand was beginning to shake. He continued, but this time with a voice less strong and forceful.

"Question every change," he said. "Challenge those who worship progress. Remember what is most important — your relationship with others, especially your family. Your connection to your community. Your relationship with God. And above all your relationship with the land. For each new machine. For each new invention you are considering buying, whether it is a new plow, a new kitchen stove, or a roll of barbed wire, ask these questions. Take time to consider the answers. Don't rush into acceptance. Go slow. Life is not a horse race. Life is not rushing toward some unknown goal. Life is a stroll, a slow walk, a chance to breathe the clean air, to stop and marvel at the wildflowers, to answer your children's questions, to feel your feet touching the earth. Remember, the best of what is next has been here all along."

Once more he drank from the glass next to him, and swabbed the perspiration from his brow. The front of his black coat was wet with sweat, and it was dripping from his nose.

"The good life is a simple life, where the little things are appreciated — a quiet word from your spouse, home grown vegetables on your table, an uninterrupted night's sleep, the smile of a little baby, the flight of wild geese winging north in the spring, the rumble of thunder on a hot night in July.

"Machines complicate our lives, take away the simple pleasures, and ultimately draw us away from the land. As we are pulled from the land, we leave behind the essence of our humanity. A life without a connection to the land is an empty life. A life filled with doing and the absence of being. I fear, oh how I fear, that we are becoming humans doing, rather than human beings.

"And so my friends," Increase Joseph said.

"Only you can act on my words. Each of you has that great responsibility to look progress and change in the eye and challenge them. Our very humanity depends on it."

Increase Joseph took a seat, drank the remainder of the contents in the glass and slid the well worn and faded Red Book back into his pocket. The audience immediately jumped to its feet, applauding loudly and cheering. Never before had he received such a response to his words. He sat with his head down, not seeming to recognize the praise he was receiving. The clapping and cheering went on, until finally Little Joe stood up and said, "Thank you all for coming."

Chapter 29
World's Fair

May 1893

The remainder of the 1880s sped by. Increase Joseph, now 67, had slowed down considerably from his earlier work schedule. Elwina was taking more time to visit with friends and sit in her rocking chair, knitting. The Links had essentially given up their meager farm operation several years ago, when the Standalone Fellowship elders voted to pay Increase Joseph a modest salary for his pastoral efforts. He promptly sold their half dozen cows, gave the hogs to Little Joe, and allowed the farm to return to its natural state, which he preferred anyway.

The traveling tent ministry continued, but on a reduced scale. Little Joe did most of the tent preaching, inviting his famous father to say a few words at the end of each program. When Little Joe's son, Little Joe Too, reached ten, he began traveling with his father and grandfather and was introduced to selling Link's Restorative Tonic off the back of the tonic wagon. Now, at 16, Little Joe Too had become a veteran of tent ministry.

Tonic sales continued growing each year, not

only because of the continued success of the tent program, but because Frederick Henke and his sons devised a mail order catalog featuring Standalone Cheese—Brick, Cheddar, and Limburger — plus an opportunity to buy the famous Restorative Tonic. Orders for the tonic poured in from all over the country — the profits of course flowed into the Tonic Helping Fund.

Henrietta Bakken Link took over the management of the *Link Lake Gazette* from her father. She expanded the business to include a commercial print shop where she printed the Standalone catalog each spring and fall. Thousands of copies were mailed to every state.

The recipe for the tonic remained a secret, known only to Increase Joseph who visited the cheese factory several times a year supervising the brewing of a new batch, but never revealing the details for the concoction.

Sunday afternoon services continued at the Standalone Church, but membership had begun to dwindle the last several years. Attendance was especially light on the Sundays when Increase Joseph was the only speaker. As he aged, his prestige in the community had diminished somewhat. Several of the younger members left the Fellowship, complaining that Increase Joseph's ideas were outdated and didn't fit a modern world.

When Increase Joseph learned the reason for their leaving, he was deeply disappointed. He believed firmly that his words were the words of the ages.

On those Sundays when Little Joe spoke, the attendance was nearly that of earlier years. Little Joe's message was essentially the same as his father's but he spoke in softer tones and in a less strident manner. Every couple of months Henrietta Link stood in the preaching pit. Her approach, which had become popular, was to start with a witticism, and then let that be the basis for a discussion.

A week ago, she spoke on the phrase, "Don't allow others to tell you what to think." The sense of those words had long been the essence of the Standalone Fellowship's philosophy, where everyone was entitled to his own opinion and had the right to express it. Henrietta's message was well accepted by everyone.

The year 1893 was not a good one. Banks were closing all across the country. Every week the *Link Lake Gazette* carried another story about how difficult times had become. Sometimes the news happened close to home. Headlines in the August 2nd edition read, "The City Bank of Portage closed last week." The brief story concluded that "The suspension is due to the condition of the money market."

Another story reported that railroad companies from one end of the country to the other were going bankrupt, and unemployment among factory workers had reached more than twenty percent. People in Link Lake began seeing haggard, defeated men stopping at their doors, begging for food, and then walking on, as if in a daze. They were called tramps, and by spring 1893 these men were everywhere. Many offered to work for a meal — splitting wood was a popular task.

Increase Joseph suggested using the Tonic Helping Fund to provide food for these poor desperate men. The Standalone Ladies Circle served free soup at the Standalone Church every noon, and men lined up as early as 11 each morning.

One of the elders suggested that the men should hear a message before they received their food. Increase Joseph said, "They have already heard a loud and terrifying message; what they need now is food." No religious message was ever offered, although the hungry men were invited to Sunday afternoon services if interested.

After Henrietta had finished helping prepare the noon lunch at the church one day in May, she stopped by the newspaper office, worked for a couple hours, and returned home to prepare supper for Little Joe and Little Joe Too. When they had finished eating, she said, "I want to read you a story we printed in this week's *Link Lake Gazette*." Henrietta could now obtain national news from the Associated Press over leased telegraph wires. Since the railroad and telegraph service had come to Plainfield, 15 miles west of Link Lake, Henrietta had access to the same news as the big urban newspapers.

"Something new this week?" Little Joe asked, yawning. "Or more gossip about who met where and what they had to eat?"

"Just listen to this," Henrietta said as she unfolded the paper and held it so the light of the kitchen lamp fell on the front page.

"World's Columbian Exposition opened in Chicago May 1. Fair celebrates the 400th anniversary of Christopher Columbus' arrival in the new world.

"One hundred thousand people watched as President Grover Cleveland pushed the golden lever that started dynamo engines generating electricity. Fairgrounds covers 633 acres, boasts 65,000 exhibits, seats 7,000 in its restaurants. Has a huge Ferris wheel, displays native villages and showcases fourteen great white buildings that surround natural waterways. The Exposition applauds the advance of American civilization. Officials said it is the greatest cultural and entertainment event in the history of the world. Fair was scheduled to open in 1892, 400 years after Columbus arrived in the Americas, but politics and construction problems delayed the opening a year."

"Isn't this wonderful?" she said as she pointed to the newspaper article. "We should go. Drive to Plainfield and take the train. No time at all we'll be in Chicago."

"What will my father think? He doesn't care much for fairs, says they stir up people and take their minds off what is important," said Little Joe.

"Tell him I need up-to-date information for the people. Our readers deserve a first hand story, not one put together by a Chicago reporter. My father and mother can handle the newspaper for a couple days; after all they took care of it for years." She turned to Little Joe Too, "You wouldn't mind taking care of the chores around the farm while we're gone, would you?"

The look on Little Joe Too's face suggested he didn't have much say in the matter.

It was clear Henrietta had made up her mind. She was going to the World's Fair in Chicago.

"I'll talk to father," Little Joe said. "I need his permission."

"Since when? Aren't you a Standalone? Aren't you entitled to follow your own mind?"

"I don't want to harm the ministry," Little Joe said. "Fairs are about new things. New things mean change, and change means people forget what is important."

"We can't stand in the way of change," said Henrietta. "And I can't act like it isn't happening. What kind of newspaper would we have if I didn't report what was going on in the world?"

"But you never question anything, Henrietta. You take everything as it comes."

"You make up for it, Little Joe. You're always questioning — from why we print the Standalone Catalog, to why I send a man to Plainfield each day for the Associated Press news." She smiled at her husband. "Want some more coffee?" she asked.

The next morning Little Joe climbed on his horse and rode the short distance to his parents' home — they still lived in the original log cabin Increase Joseph built when they came to Ames County in 1852, although they had added two rooms.

He found his father sitting in his usual place, the preaching pit of the church, deeply engrossed in the Red Book. Upon hearing the door open, the senior Link looked up.

"I've come to see you, Father," said Little Joe as he walked toward the center of the church.

"How are you my son, on this glorious day?"

"I have a matter I must discuss with you," Little Joe said.

"I am always prepared for discussion," Increase Joseph replied. His long white hair had thinned somewhat in past years.

"It concerns Henrietta and me," Little Joe said hesitantly.

"Oh, the challenges of matrimony. We who are married all have these problems."

"Henrietta wants to go to the World's Fair in Chicago."

"For what reason? Fairs put troubling thoughts in people's minds."

"I know, Father. I know. I told her that. But she still insists on going; says her readers deserve first hand information."

"She's a strong minded woman, son, intelligent, but strong minded."

"Henrietta says we must change our ministry, bring it more up to date, talk about progress and embrace change more than we have. She may be right. We have been losing members lately, you know. Some have said we are out of date."

"Those who have left have not heeded our message, Little Joe. They have not heard our words."

Henrietta wants me to go with her to Chicago," Little Joe blurted out.

"You, of course, said no."

"I'm going, Father. She won't change her mind. She can't go alone. It is my duty as her husband to go with her."

"I am disappointed, son. Disappointed," The man in black turned back to the Red Book without looking up as Little Joe, his head down, walked toward the church door and out into the bright sunlight of a June morning.

Two days later Henry Bakken drove his daughter and son-in-law in his buggy to the depot in Plainfield where they caught the Portage Branch of the Wisconsin Central Railroad for their trip to Chicago — it would be their first train ride. The train rolled by fields of grazing dairy cattle, traveled through the marshlands near Endeavor and Portage, and in a short time arrived in Madison, the state capital and the largest city they had so far visited.

A few hours later they were in Chicago, that smelly, growing metropolis tucked up against Lake Michigan. They looked for evidence of the great Chicago fire of 1871 that occurred the same day that Peshtigo burned, but they saw no remnants as the buildings had been rebuilt.

Soon they arrived at the exposition grounds which had previously been marshy and little-used Jackson Park. Both stood outside the entrance and looked at the mass of people entering the fairgrounds.

"Isn't this wonderful?" said Henrietta.

Little Joe shook his head in disbelief, for he never imagined such a thing as he was seeing. There were beautiful buildings and an enormous wheel that carried people high up into the air. Lighted electrical bulbs were everywhere. Would electric bulbs replace kerosene lamps and lanterns?

As they walked from building to building, they saw new things to buy: Cream of Wheat, Shredded Wheat, Aunt Jemima Syrup, Juicy Fruit Gum, prize winning Pabst beer.

Henrietta wanted to try everything, taste it, smell it, and feel it. She furiously took notes as they saw exhibit after exhibit. Little Joe was mostly numb. Never in his life had he encountered so many different and exotic things.

They strolled through the midway where they found vendors selling food and trinkets of every stripe. They saw a marching band that someone said was playing John Philip Sousa's work. They listened to a young piano player pounding out music they had never heard before — ragtime it was called. They learned the young man's name was Scott Joplin.

When they stopped for lunch, they drank carbonated soda water, and ate hamburgers — both new to them. They learned that the hamburger was discovered by a short order cook in Seymour, Wisconsin, who at an 1885 local fair determined that fairgoers could more easily eat their meatballs if he made them portable by putting them between two slices of bread.

They visited Buffalo Bill's Wild West, a show just outside the fairgrounds where Buffalo Bill Cody and his entourage of cowboys and Indians tried to replicate the old West. Hundreds of people watched in amazement.

They saw works of art, paintings and sculptures. And they listened to speakers extol the wonderful future for urban life with its vast cultural and educational opportunities. As they walked by a lecture hall they heard a tall bearded man proclaim, "The United States is moving from an agrarian to an industrial society. Technology is king and progress has become America's destiny."

Henrietta quickly scribbled the quotation in her notebook. All day she asked questions, conducted interviews, and recorded the answers in her note pad.

She and Little Joe spent the night in Chicago, not sleeping well because the sounds of the city never ceased. Something was happening all night, and most of it made noise—whistles, teamsters yelling at horses, water running, unknown deep throated rumbling sounds.

The following morning they climbed back on the train and headed north. For several miles they sat quietly, alone with their thoughts. Henrietta was paging through her voluminous notes, no doubt framing in her mind the several articles she planned to write.

"Wasn't it wonderful?" Henrietta finally said, breaking the silence.

"No," said Little Joe, curtly. "No, it wasn't."

"How can you say that?"

"Because it is true"

They rode on in silence for several miles.

"What didn't you like?" Henrietta finally asked quietly.

"All the talk about technology and progress. It sounds like progress is the religion of the machine, the ministry of big business and the worship of want."

"It's the future, Joe, It's the future."

"No one talked about the land and how we depend on and are tied to it. Not one person. Not one word. Not a mention. All I heard was progress, progress, progress — and the need to leave behind old ideas and old ways of thinking."

"We can't stand in the way of progress, Joe," she said, looking with concern at her husband.

"But we will be doomed; we will all be doomed unless we listen to the land."

"That's an old way of thinking, Joe."

"It is not," said Little Joe, bristling. "How can we ever accept that city life is better than living in the country? It's blasphemous."

"Joe, Joe, you're getting all excited." She placed her hands on his and looked into his eyes.

"Cities," Little Joe said, "are pig sties where

people live on top of each other, never see the setting sun and seldom hear a bird sing. City people have forgotten, if they ever knew, the smell of newly turned soil, the sound of rain drumming on a barn roof, the sight of a new calf nursing its mother, the feel of a summer breeze after a day of hard work."

"Oh, Joe," Henrietta said. She turned to look out the train window, past the farmers working in their fields, past the horses and cows in the green pastures, past the wagons and buggies waiting at the rail crossings. No further words passed between them as the train rumbled north.

Chapter 30
Transition

Henry Bakken met Henrietta and Little Joe at the train depot in Plainfield and they rode back to Link Lake, along vast potato fields that were recently planted and hayfields that would soon be ready for cutting

"How was the fair?" Bakken inquired.

"Wonderful," his daughter answered. "Simply wonderful. And look at this." She showed her father her notebook that was crammed full of writing. "I have enough material for a half dozen articles, maybe more."

As they rode, Little Joe remained silent, alone with his thoughts and the memory of the bitter exchange he'd had with his wife. While Henrietta was talking, Little Joe thought about his need to talk with his father.

Once they were home and unpacked, Little Joe told Henrietta he must visit Increase Joseph. When he arrived at the Link cabin, he spotted his mother sitting on the front porch, in her rocking chair.

"Where is father?" Little Joe asked.

"Gone for a walk. He does that a lot lately. I worry about him. He thinks all his work has been for naught, that people are ignoring his message," Elwina said.

"I know," said Little Joe. "It is a great worry of his. I must reassure him that he is right, no matter what others are saying and doing. Which way did he go?"

"Probably to his favorite place, under the big oak tree back of the church where he can see the lake."

As Little Joe left the cabin, he noticed a menacing bank of black clouds that had quickly come up in the west and was rolling across Link Lake. He hurried toward the oak tree that he could see in the distance. A figure of a man sat under it, scarcely visible. Flashes of lightning tore across the blackening sky as Little Joe hurried toward the tree. Thunder shook the ground. Little Joe expected his father to get up and head back toward the cabin to avoid being drenched. But the man in black did not move.

"Father," Little Joe called. "Father, the storm! The storm!" But the famous preacher did not respond.

The first big drops of rain splattered in the dust of the dim trail that led to the giant oak. A gust of cold wind was followed by the rumble of nearby thunder. Little Joe pulled his black hat down hard to keep it from blowing off.

Rain began falling as if God himself were pouring barrels of water on the landscape. Rivulets of water began gushing down the trail.

A simultaneous flash of lightning and deafening thunder nearly threw Little Joe to the ground. For a moment he was stunned by the earth-shaking report. He looked toward the oak tree and his father. Through the pouring rain, he glimpsed a huge white gap that had opened in the top of the ancient tree. His father continued to sit under it, like a black statue.

"Father, Father," Little Joe called as he ran in the rain toward the tree.

"Father," he called again. "Father!"

His famous father sat with his eyes open, looking through the rain toward the lake. Water ran from the brim of his black hat and dripped on his long white fingers that held the Red Book.

"Father," Little Joe said again, this time quietly. But he knew there would be no answer. Tears welled up in his eyes. He took the Red Book from his father's hands and shoved it in his own pocket, out of the weather.

Little Joe knelt in front of his father and began talking through his tears.

"Father, you were correct, as you have always been. You warned me about what I would hear in Chicago. You've long known that change and progress were overtaking us, and we must be aware of the consequences. But your warning became a whisper, a quiet voice in the stampede of shouts about progress no matter what the consequences. Oh, Father, you must hear me. I beg forgiveness for doubting you.

"I've turned over and over in my mind your words spoken just last week. You said, 'No matter how fast things change, hold on to those that don't.' You have reminded us in a hundred ways that there can be no true progress without respecting land, without people respecting each other, without worshiping a loving God that gives us the freedom to make our own decisions."

The rain was letting up. The hillside where Little Joe knelt beside his father was an expanse of new green grass. Splinters of oak wood, a reminder of lightning's power, were scattered among the brilliant blue lupines.

"Oh, Father," Little Joe sobbed. His black coat was even blacker as it became soaked in rain. "Why did I question you? Your words never wavered from the truth.   I will never question the wisdom of the Red Book again."

The sun broke from the clouds. Little Joe picked up his father and began the short walk to the church. Elwina Link, who had been watching from the cabin porch, saw Little Joe carrying her husband into the round church. She grabbed up a shawl and ran toward her son and husband.

"Is he hurt? Is he hurt?" she screamed.

"He is gone," Little Joe said, "Our spiritual leader is dead."

"Oh, no," Elwina gasped as she ran her fingers over the wrinkled face of her husband. "Oh, no!"

Henrietta, on her way to the Link cabin in search of Little Joe, saw him carrying the man in black into the church. She ran down the hill to her parent's house where she summoned Henry and Abigail.

Others soon gathered at the church, where Little Joe placed Increase Joseph's body in the preaching pit — a place he thought fitting.

"Is he . . . is he dead?" Henry asked when he saw his old friend lying prone.

"Yes . . . my father has left us," Little Joe said. He had great difficulty speaking as tears were pouring down his face.

"You are now our leader," said Henry Bakken

quietly. Bakken too fought back tears for he and his old friend had been through so much over the years.

"Do you have the Red Book?" Bakken inquired.

Little Joe reached for the famed Red Book from his inside pocket. It was faded; its pages tattered and damp at the edges. He opened the book carefully with those around unable to see inside it.

"Read from it, Little Joe," Henry said. No one except Increase Joseph had been privy to the contents of the book that guided the Standalone Fellowship all these years.

Through his tears, Little Joe began paging through the sacred book. He noted that every page was blank; the only writing was on the inside back cover, "Recipe for the tonic in a box behind the dill pickles in the pantry."

Little Joe stood up straight, cleared his throat and selected a page near the front of the book. He read aloud, "The **Land** comes first."

Acknowledgments

I especially want to thank Marv Balousek, former owner of Badger Books, who took a chance by publishing this, my first novel, and encouraging me to do more fiction.

I also want to thank the University of Wisconsin Press, and especially senior acquisitions editor Raphael Kadushin, for agreeing to publish the paperback version of this novel and for encouraging me to write the additional novels that have become known as my Ames County series.

Special thanks go to my daughter, Sue, an elementary school teacher and a reading specialist who read several drafts of this book and offered important ideas for both character and plot development. Sue reads with a critical eye for detail, but also has an uncanny ability to see the bigger picture of a story with all its warts and problems.

Matt Apps, my nephew and a businessman, read several drafts of the book. I made several important changes in both the structure and focus of the book based on his suggestions. My son Jeff, a banker in Colorado, is a no nonsense reader of my work, both my nonfiction and fiction. He helped with the title for the book and with fine-tuning the focus. My oldest son, Steve, a photo-journalist, reads all of my material and focuses on the larger purpose of a project. In addition to invaluable help with the broader sweeps of the story, when I was ready to throw in the towel on the project he kept encouraging me to keep on. My patient and seemingly never-tiring wife reads all of my material, from the earliest, roughest drafts to later, more polished versions. With her suggestion, several of my first chapter attempts found their way into the wastepaper basket.

I want to express a long overdue gratitude to August Derleth, who wrote many popular fiction and nonfiction books about Wisconsin. It was in one of Derleth's writing workshops at the School of the Arts in Rhinelander in 1967 where I learned some of the basics of fiction writing from a master novelist. August Derleth died too early in 1971.

And finally, thanks to my old friend and mentor, Robert Gard (also deceased), who got me started writing books, helped me publish my first book in 1970, and never wavered in his support of my work.

To all of these people and many more I owe a debt of gratitude. Although book writing is a solitary endeavor, in one way or another many people look over your shoulder. How great that they do.